I0684287

SPIRITS IN YOUR AREA

- the anthology -

Jonathan E. Furneaux

Spirits in Your Area

Copyright © 2020 by Jonathan E. Furneaux

All rights reserved. This book or any portion thereof may not be reproduced or used in any manner whatsoever without the express written permission of the publisher except for the use of brief quotations in a book review.

Independently Published
ISBN: 978-0-6487696-1-3

www.jonathanfurneaux.com

For Oma.
May we meet again.

Table of Contents

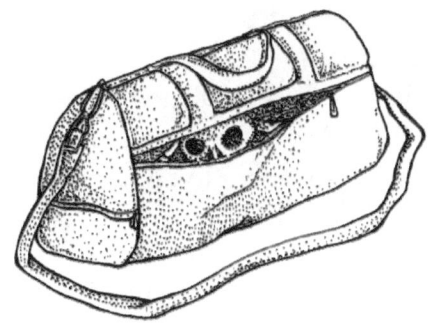

Sound the Sirens

I stopped for petrol at the service station, which was nestled beneath the highway overpass. It was midnight, and the station's exterior was only illuminated by the orange lights of overhead streetlamps, and the occasional white-hot flash of a car rudely rounding the bend with its high-beams on.

I'd been listening to Cream on the radio as they crooned about someone named Ulysses. I killed the engine, ending Eric Clapton's psychedelic guitar.

The stranger who caught my eye was leaning against the brickwork of the service station while she smoked an unfiltered cigarette. She waited beneath the cashier's window, right under his nose. Her feet were hoisted up on her gym bag.

As I went past to pay, she was humming Clapton's guitar riff, and when I stepped outside again, she'd started another cigarette. The smoke from her breath was a blue-grey acid in the cold evening air. Her hair was the colour of traffic cones and construction tape.

"You like Clapton?" I asked, taking a chance as the station's glass doors met behind me. "I've been hooked on far too much prog-rock recently. I was about to call you Aphrodite."

She smiled, and she carefully examined my legs.

"Are you waiting for someone?" I asked.

"The only person I need is right here," she stood and stretched. "Which way are you heading?"

As she stretched, her cigarette hand rose like the fist of Lady Liberty. The service station worker tapped the frosted class with a knuckle, and waved an index finger at the cigarette. Aphrodite waved a different finger back in reply.

"I'm going home to Gympie," I said.

"What a coincidence." She leant down slowly, and collected her gym bag. Its contents clicked and clacked. The last thing she collected was a large canister of petrol. "I'm going that same direction."

The air was frigid, but my heater was far too effective. My old Corolla coughed along the Bruce Highway as I stomped the clutch and slapped the long gear stick back to third. Then I switched the heater off.

The stranger slept peacefully through the rises and dips of the road, curled up with her back to me. Her gym bag sat in the back.

I hadn't seen another car for half an hour, and the highway was beginning to look unfamiliar. It became thickly forested on either side, which I didn't recall from my last trip home. I thought about stopping for the night, but I hadn't seen an exit for ages. Besides, I'd promised to take her as far as Gympie.

I checked my wristwatch; it was one o'clock. The painted lines of the highway had vanished, and now my single-working headlight was the only light winking for kilometres. I waited until my teeth began to chatter, and then blasted the heater until it became unbearable again.

The girl slept on.

Her long, orange hair fell from her head in perfectly straight sheets, like a veil. She was an athlete, perhaps. Her calves and thighs were firm and shapely, and stretched the fabric of her torn jeans. She'd taken off her canvas shoes the second she'd climbed into the passenger seat: kicked them off before she'd even adjusted her seatbelt.

I smiled despite myself. She seemed cute, and I'd enjoyed our brief conversation before she'd politely retired to sleep. Apparently, she was on her way home, and she hadn't mentioned anyone special.

There was a small part of me that inevitably began to imagine some sort of future with her. Perhaps I'd invite her to a bar. She might give me her number. I'd done her the courtesy of driving her all the way to Gympie, so it'd be the least she could do. Maybe she'd wake up and tell me to stop driving for the night. We could take some sleeping bags I keep in the back, and go sleep in the forest under the stars.

I held the steering wheel with my knees and rubbed my hands together for warmth. I flicked the heater from *non-existent*, back to *volcanic*. A large beam of light swept across the road.

I grabbed the wheel.

The strange light silhouetted the tree canopy, and then blinded me through my side mirror. Ahead, I could see other white-hot beams of light scouring the road and surrounding land: helicopters, most likely. I nudged the girl awake, and she groaned into existence.

"Bugger," was all she could manage, rubbing her face. "I was afraid of this."

I chanced a look at her then, averting my gaze from the road. Her veil of hair had parted. She leaned close to the glass to stare up at the lights in the sky. Her eyes were impossibly large: blue irises glistening, even in the pale illumination of the headlight. She was a vision, pieced together from the list called: *my ideal girl.*

"They found us."

"Someone's looking for you?" I asked. The lights were coming closer.

"Yes and no," she said, and pulled her hair across one shoulder. "They're looking for you...I'm sorry, I've forgotten your name."

I applied the brakes, and pulled over.

"Yeah, good idea," she said. "We've got a lot to talk about."

I turned off the engine, and my working headlight. One of the spotlights approached from a few kilometres away, glancing along valleys and around hills.

"They're after me? I doubt it."

"Well, more specifically, they don't want *you* to be with *me*," the girl said. "They can't really touch me yet. I don't leave much evidence, you see, but they can try and snatch anyone who's with me."

4

"I'm sorry," I said. "I don't follow what's happening here. Is it the police? The army?"

I looked back at the approaching light, but as it drew closer, I began to doubt that it was even a helicopter after all. It was too close to the ground, too stable in the sky. Too certain and dexterous as it moved above the trees.

She watched me with a raised eyebrow, while I scanned the sky.

"It's not the cops," she said. "It looks like you can see into the spirit world."

I laughed at that. I couldn't help it. The light above disappeared for a moment, and then swept along the length of road we had just pulled off. In the rear-view, I saw the beam sweep a hundred metres in a second. The source was nearly above us.

"Well, whether you believe it or not doesn't particularly bother me," she said, in almost a deadpan. Reaching down, she began to pull her shoes on.

A white beam of light hit the bonnet of my car. There was something primal in me that flinched from its starkness. It was the same instinct that makes animals freeze on the road: a sudden confrontation of light, which causes innocent men to run.

"Well," she said, talking through a yawn. "You'll believe in spirits pretty soon, regardless."

"Should we run?" I asked, but I already doubted that I could manage it.

"Sure, we could try that." She reached over to the seat behind her, and grabbed her gym bag. The light somehow grew brighter still, and then flicked away suddenly. A loud screech tore the air. It sounded like steel being twisted.

"It's signalling the others," she nodded towards my window. "That guardian will wait for backup."

I craned my neck around to see.

It was outside.

The creature stood above the tree canopy easily. It was at least ten metres tall. As it approached the car, I saw its legs. They fell to the ground like a hundred spools of impossibly red string. The fibres billowed and swayed, as if in a breeze, and the head of the creature was carried along by them. There was no body to speak of, just a single orifice and rows of small beady black eyes that surrounded the maw. It had teeth like a whale: long, comb-like teeth, which bristled out from deep in its throat.

I'd always thought that in a life-or-death situation I'd have the guts to act, but I was wrong. I felt something warm, and I looked down to see that I'd wet myself. There was no sensation in my feet. Something cold and uncomfortable had been inserted into the back of my neck and the pit of my stomach.

The creature outside finished its roar with a gurgle, and then a large, illuminated proboscis extended out of its mouth, alighting the road once again.

The girl sat with her bag ready. She shook her head pitifully at the puddle in my lap.

"Well, I think I might head into the bush and give this guy the slip." She undid her seatbelt, and I suddenly found the resolve to grab her slender arm as she kicked the door open.

"Please, take me with you," I begged. "Don't leave me here with it."

She grinned. "You're coming with. I don't want to lose

those legs of yours."

She was strong. She leant across, undid my seatbelt, and pulled me from my chair, across the handbrake, and out into the frigid air. The creature behind us bellowed loudly again. It was answered by two other howls close by. Aphrodite slung her gym bag over her shoulder. She grabbed the canister of fuel in one hand, and then pulled me by arm with the other hand. Her long, pink nails dug in sharply.

We reached the tree line and then we were past it, weaving between the trunks as I willed my legs to work properly. Something had locked inside my right kneecap, so I couldn't bend it properly. I looked down and saw that it had been bent slightly outward when Aphrodite had dragged me from the car. She led us deeper into the trees. The red strings tumbled along as the creature gained on us.

"What is that thing?" I managed to gasp as I half-ran, half-limped behind her.

"It's a guardian," she called back. "They can choose to transform into a spirit, and back again."

She deftly dodged underneath a low-hanging tree limb. Its spiked bark caught me in the face and tore the soft skin around my left eye as I failed to duck.

"Slow down," I moaned, but she kept running.

"There's the forces of order and chaos," she said, effortlessly changing direction suddenly to avoid a beam of light that swept past us a few metres on the right. I, however, was whipped about by the course correction, and my neck jerked suddenly. There was a loud click, and a sharp pain. I couldn't turn my head.

"There are spirits that protect humans, and those that

want to harm them."

Up ahead, I could see a fallen tree in the moonlight. Its roots were splayed out like a forgotten umbrella. She ran towards it. As we approached the fallen tree, I saw that there was a small gap between the earth and the rotting wood. The girl looked around quickly, before ushering me through the gap with a shove. Her eyes were glistening with excitement in the moonlight.

I fell under the tree, and into a small hovel dug there by nature long ago. Wet loam covered the ground. It teemed with insects. The girl scurried through behind me and dropped her bag. Something like a xylophone clicked inside.

Despite being pulled along like a ragdoll, I felt a sense of exhilaration. She was on the run from something, so she'd need someone to watch her back. I'd be the guy she could depend on. We would collapse together tonight and sleep, and then hit the road again. It was a life of adventure and hijinks awaiting us: I could taste it.

"We won't be disturbed down here," she said, smiling.

I admired her while I forced my breathing to slow. Even though she was muscular, there was a delicate grace and strength about her. We'd probably be very happy together.

"Where was I?" she asked. "Oh yes, so the guardians want to stop me from meeting men, such as yourself, and killing them."

My mind reeled when I heard the plural: men. Did that mean tonight wasn't special for her? Was I just another guy?

"It's nothing personal," she said, apologetically. "I've got to kill you, because I need your body to help my boyfriend."

"What did you say?" I asked, hoping that I'd

misunderstood her.

"I have a boyfriend," she repeated with a sheepish shrug. She unzipped the gym bag, and inside I saw the skull of a human. It was covered by a red and blue spiralled pattern. The sockets of the skull's eyes glowed a faint green.

Damn, I thought. *I'd be a way better boyfriend for her.*

She must have seen the disappointment on my face. "Sorry. We've been together since high school."

I shrugged. "Oh no, it's completely fine. I wasn't trying to crack onto you or anything. I just figured you needed some help with those tall spirit things."

"It's a shame you didn't just wait in the car a few moments longer," she said, patting me on the head to reinforce our friendship. Then she dug out a long, curved blade, and skewered me through the heart with it.

"Those guardians out there would have pulled you to safety once they surrounded me. They're so very dedicated to protecting humans. It's a shame about the appearance really. Sorry, hold still, I need your legs."

She pushed me down, and sat on my chest. I heard a cracking sound, and I realised she had expertly dislocated my femur. I relaxed and let the pain swell over me.

"Oh, Richard," she said, laughing at the skull. "Stop it, you'll make me blush."

Before the darkness of unconsciousness enveloped me, I thought about telling her how beautiful her laugh was. If things with her boyfriend don't work out, I might do it.

9

Miscellaneous

Winter had been arduous and unforgiving, but our master was far worse. He now spent most mornings alone, sitting in the dim light of the castle's banquet hall. It was by far the coldest room in the estate.

Boards of timber covered the broken windows and shards of stained-glass littered the royal carpet, hinting at how grand the room must have once been. The brass candle sconces now drooped with beards of candle wax. The gold-trimmed wallpapers had been slashed by something sharp, and many oil portraits had been tossed into the courtyard and burned on a pyre before we could see them.

Our master was hairy.

His chest and back were thick, black carpets, and his beard was full and long, falling proudly to his knees. We were thankful for that, because the master also refused to wear anything other than a stained, woollen cloak that he wrapped around himself in the frigid cold of winter.

The fireplace was empty. The stockpile of wood that the castle once had, was now being used to barricade the gates and bar the windows. The master had felled every tree in the garden this past week, and used the wood to reinforce the grand front doors from the inside.

"Bring me entertainment!" he screamed at the darkness.

We'd drawn straws, and an unfortunate candelabra was pushed out of the shadows by the rest of us.

"Master," it said in a voice like squeaking metal. "I'd like to sing a song I wrote about the winter."

"Bah!" the master threw a cold leg of chicken in the candelabra's direction. "I hate winter. Why would you write a song about that?"

"P-please master," the candlestick stammered, climbing up onto the table with shaking arms. "I don't remember any of the other seasons. I'm just writing what I know."

The master glared at the candelabra beneath his unkempt eyebrows, and suddenly he smiled a warm invitation. "Never you mind that," he said, and gestured the candelabra over.

It looked back towards us, and then back at the master.

"Come on," the master said. He leaned forward from the shadows, and his face was illuminated by the moonlight. "Don't be afraid little guy."

The candelabra hopped on his base towards the master, until he was within reach.

"There, now I can see you better. Why don't you do a little dance for me instead?"

"O-of course master," it said. To the candelabra's credit, he did do a fair imitation of what I imagine dancing would look like. However, he misjudged a step, and landed on the edge of a plate. It upended, spilling cold peas and gravy across the table, and onto the master's lap.

Far away in the night, an owl cried. The kettle beside me turned and hopped away, unable to watch. The candelabra was apologising profusely, and leaned forward to try and scrape the gravy off the master's bare thighs. The gargantuan man simply wrapped a large hand around the candelabra's stem. Another hand grasped its head firmly.

"No, please no!" the candelabra screamed.

There was a loud cracking sound, and the candelabra's shrill screams were suddenly cut short. The candelabra's spirit, in the shape of an overweight man with a moustache, wafted through the air and evaporated from sight. The footstool and teapot quickly turned and left the scene as well. I followed at a hop, my pages flapping quietly.

But not the chamber pot.

The chamber pot remained, and watched everything like he always did. Another loud crack echoed through the halls of our home.

* * *

We all gathered in the room furthest from the master's sleeping chambers. Timber scraped, metal clanged, and porcelain chimed as everyone tried to speak at once.

"We have to escape tonight!" a broom swept.

"He'll kill us all before winter ends!" the teapot steeped.

"Enough!" I yelled above the din. "Even from this distance, I'm sure you'll wake the master."

The room fell silent.

"Now, we all knew a month ago that something had to be done." I said. My statement was met with the approximation of nodding. "That was confirmed by the first death. No one here wants any more suffering."

More nodding.

"However, I don't think running away is the best course of action. Now, now—" I quickly added, raising my voice above the objections. "—hear me out. How far could we possibly get as a group? Not all of us were blessed with handles or wooden legs to move about with. If we try a mass exodus, the master will figure it out the very next morning. He'll find us easily: a hundred objects running through the mountain snow won't be easily missed. Once he finds us, what do you think he'll do?"

"Let's just kill him first!" the kettle hissed. There were several others in agreement.

"You've forgotten what happened last time we tried that," I said simply. "He now spends the nights alone, with an axe under his arm in that empty bedroom. We'd have to force our way in, and he'd hear us. No offense, but the heaviest of us, the ones who could do some real damage, are also the loudest and slowest. It'd be a suicide mission, and I'm firmly against that. Besides, he barely sleeps from what the chamber pot tells me."

"Speak of the devil," someone huffed.

The chamber pot slunk into the room like a wounded animal. He had one handle, and because his porcelain was so wide and low, he was forced to drag and scrape himself along the ground with it.

14

The chamber pot was the least-popular of the household servants. He was also the only servant allowed within the restricted wing of the castle that held the master's bedroom. Each night, the chamber pot would wait outside the locked door for any nightly emergencies. This meant that he was privy to most of the master's rants and lunacy throughout the night.

It had changed him over the winter.

Many said that they couldn't stand the chamber pot because of his cold and callous demeanour. I do think that was partly to blame. It was probably also the stench.

"What are you doing here?" I asked. "If the master finds you missing, he'll come to investigate."

The chamber pot ignored my question and addressed the group instead. "I've got information." He paused for dramatic effect. "I think I know how we turned into these objects."

"How? When did you find that out?" I asked.

"Well, unlike you all, I've been thinking long and hard about our predicament," said the chamber pot. "How come we can't remember anything before winter began? How come we all came to life in the master's bedroom? Why does this castle look like it was attacked and looted? How come this particular book is alive—" he gestured with his handle to me, "—and the others aren't?"

"Are you going to tell us, or not?"

The chamber pot crawled to the centre of the room, urine splashing onto the carpet as he did so. "I decided to stick around after the master pulled the candelabra to pieces."

"What an awful thing to peep on," someone chimed in.

"So, the master kills the candelabra. He finishes his meal, and tosses the fellow out the window. Then he goes through

15

the kitchen, and I lose sight of him. He comes back, and he's been down to the wine cellar. So, I start my journey up towards his room, and I get there by the time he's gone for a third bottle. He comes up and takes a squat on me just before bed. While he's sitting there, he must've forgotten who he was, because he starts rambling."

"Get on with it," I said with a sigh.

"He keeps saying 'stupid witch' over and over. Gets into a real mantra with it. He says that he 'could've been something great', and that 'my men are furniture now', and then he laughs into the air."

"That furniture is us?" I asked.

"It's us," the chamber pot replied. "So, I take it that means we used to be men, like him."

"Who is this witch then?"

"That's the best bit, isn't it?" he said with a smug smile. "See, just inside the master's bedroom, there's one portrait that he didn't burn. He likes to spit on it. Tonight, he was talking to that picture, while he sat on me."

"Do you suppose that this 'witch' woman in the picture is the one who turned us into these objects?" I asked.

"That'd make sense, wouldn't it?"

"Well then," I said, trying to wrestle back control of the meeting, "we find out the identity of this lady, then we find her, and get her to turn us back into men like the master!"

A cheer went up from the objects assembled there, but it was interrupted by the chamber pot shouting over the top. "You didn't let me finish, book," he said. "I already know her name."

"How?"

The chamber pot shrugged with his handle. "Her name was engraved under the portrait: Poubelle."

There was a confused silence for a moment.

"I can read," the chamber pot explained.

That threw me, and it was a revelation that stirred the room into excited chatter. Up until this point, we had thought I was the only one who was literate.

"This is marvellous news," the wardrobe said. "The chamber pot can go down into the village, find this witch, and ask her to see reason."

"There's two big problems with that plan," I interjected. "Firstly, none of us has been down to the village. We've only glimpsed it through the snow. They might be used to talking objects, but they might not be. In fact, I think it's very likely that we're in a unique predicament here: we all know in our souls there's something very unnatural about us. You can see it on the master's face. Secondly, if the chamber pot goes down to the village and the master doesn't see him the next night, he'll know something is amiss. I'll sneak down to the master's quarters and study the picture for myself, and then the chamber pot doesn't have to go."

"I do have to go," he said, turning to face me. "You can't stop me."

"Be reasonable," I said. "You're not just putting yourself at risk if you leave your station. The master could very well torture other servants in order to find out where you are."

"I'm going," the chamber pot said. "You seem to like lists, so let me give you three reasons why."

I forced myself to stay calm, but there was something in the chamber pot's demeanour that rifled my pages.

17

"First, a quick glance at a picture in the dark isn't going to help you identify this Poubelle. I've studied her face every night for the past month while the master slept or ranted. It's burned into my memory. I could recognise her even if she were a hundred years old now. Second, I have the most to gain if we succeed, and the least to lose if we don't."

The smell from the chamber pot was overwhelming, and we all knew what he meant.

"Sure, but..." I struggled to think of a rebuttal.

The chamber pot made a tutting sound. "Are you actually worried about helping us? Or are you afraid of losing the power you've gained over the others?"

"How dare you—"

"—Third, I have a good idea of where Poubelle might be. I've spent weeks pouring over dead books and maps in the castle library. At first, I assumed Poubelle was a common name. I figured she must have been an ex-lover, so I never connected the dots. It was only tonight when he started rambling about 'us' and 'her' that I realised how important she was in all of this. And, I now realise that I've read that name before, on an old map of this very mountain. Here's the clincher: there's a spot on this very mountain named after her. It's a little hunting lodge or something."

"How far away is it?" the kettle asked.

"It's close enough that I could leave after breakfast, and be back before dinner."

The rest of the household looked between us expectantly. If I refused to let the chamber pot go, it would look like I was envious of him, and I was.

"Very well," I agreed. "However, I'll be coming with."

18

The chamber pot made a rude noise, the sort of noise that belongs in a chamber pot. "Why, are you afraid I'll run away?"

"I'm very concerned about that, yes," I said. "There's a reason we've stationed servants at the back door of the castle. If one of us tries to escape, well, you can remember how the master responds to that."

"Fine," the chamber pot said. A crack in his glaze resembled a smile. "I doubt the master would notice your absence."

"Wait a second," said a broom in the middle of the crowd, "you could both decide to leave us here and escape."

"We could invite two more members," I said. "You can choose amongst yourselves who you'd like to send."

They began to argue, and I hopped over to where the chamber pot was.

"Are you happy?" I asked quietly, my leather smile fixed in place. "I'll entertain this little excursion of yours, but don't try anything funny while we're out there."

The chamber pot patted my spine roughly with his handle, and I had to dodge away from the contents of his sloshing pot.

"So, will you give me a hint about where we're going?"

"No," he replied, and began dragging himself back towards the master's bedroom. "Meet me in the larder tomorrow. We'll leave via the back door during breakfast."

* * *

The next morning, four of us crept through the larder, and out into the frosted castle grounds. Last night the broom had loudly elected himself, which had been supported by the other cleaning servants. A chair volunteered, but we decided it might draw attention. The footstool was selected instead. He was dating the teapot, so he'd want to return.

A small drain was set against the castle's fortifications, which allowed freshwater to flow into the garden during the summer. The footstool had the most trouble getting past the iron bars that guarded the drain. He nearly dislocated his back legs trying to squeeze through. Once he was past, we all waded through the small river's slush, under the wall, and suddenly we were free.

A new dusting of snow had fallen during the night. A large clump of it dropped from the pine branches above, startling us as it landed with a wet thud.

The chamber pot became fairly chipper once the footstool offered to carry him on its cushioned top.

"How kind of you," said the chamber pot.

"I'm not being kind," the footstool replied. "You're just too slow."

We circled the castle walls, and then the chamber pot pointed up the mountain. "Thatta' way."

The sun reflected brightly from the white snow. It was peaceful, I realised. The creaking and sobbing of household servants had now been replaced by the quiet song of birds and the babble of a nearby stream.

Scaling the mountain was far more difficult than the chamber pot had made it out to be. The footstool was the most mobile out of all of us, but he was carrying extra weight. We climbed for several hours, circling the mountain to make the ascent more agreeable.

* * *

The master reclined at the banquet table after breakfast. The remains of his roast duck, winter vegetables, toast and milk were spread out in front of him. He stood, and peered out between the wooden boards that barred the window. The stream that fed the garden below had begun to thaw beneath the unblemished pale blue sky. The village below was quiet. Small plumes of grey smoke rose on the wind.

At the start of winter, many villagers had knocked on the gates, begging to know what had happened to their loved ones.

Your loved ones died when we took the castle, I'm so sorry, he had said. *There's nothing left to bury.*

"Do you see that?" he asked the teapot.

"What's that, master?"

"Winter is ending."

The trade routes through the mountains would also thaw. The village and this castle would be connected to the outside world once again.

"I'm in a good mood, teapot," the master said, breathing deeply. "I think I'll have my pipe this morning as well."

"I'll bring it to you at once," the teapot replied.

The master hummed as he walked to the drawing room. In the periphery of his vision, he could see the furniture and knick-knacks of the house slink further into the shadows as he passed.

Good. At the beginning of winter, there had been two clumsy attempts on his life. Now, the servants stayed far out of his way, unless he needed them.

His drawing room was warmer. It caught the morning sun, and still boasted double-glazed windows. He splayed his legs out comfortably as he reclined in his reading chair, and waited for his pipe. The teapot returned, with his pipe protruding from its spout.

21

The master retrieved it, and the teapot waited while he fiddled with his tinderbox. He struck the flint successfully, and was soon puffing on the pipe. His nostrils filled with the warm earthy scent.

"That's the good, imported stuff," he said appreciatively, and stretched out his bare legs in front of him.

"Footstool?"

There was a brief pause, so he called out again.

"Footstool!"

"I'll bring you a chair, master," the teapot said quickly, and began to hop towards the door. She had nearly escaped, when the master crossed the room in a flash, and closed the door with his foot.

"Why would I want a chair, when I asked for the footstool?"

"Apologies master," the teapot replied. "I'll just go and find him for you."

The door remained shut. The master returned to his chair, and cocked a leg over the armrest. "Come here teapot," he said quietly.

A brass door handle stood solemnly above the teapot, well out of her reach. The master basked in the sunlight. The teapot waited, its lid rattling with nerves. A stack of dirty porcelain plates sat beside the master's chair.

"Where is the footstool?" he asked.

"I don't know, master," the teapot said. She jumped as a plate smashed against the wooden door behind her.

The master retrieved another plate. "How many plates could I hit you with, before you cracked, and your spirit leaked out?" he asked.

The teapot tried to remain calm, but her body still shook.

"P-please," she begged. "I don't know anything."

"You do know something," the master replied. "Why am I so certain? It's because of your lid, teapot. It's a dead giveaway. It rattles when you're lying, and it's why I keep you around." The master leant forward, and picked the shaking teapot up. "Perhaps if you watch me break a few of the living plates, you'll talk?"

He stood, opened the door, and called for a plate. That was when the teapot started talking. It came slowly at first, but then the words tumbled out faster and faster, muddled with apologies and pleas for mercy.

* * *

The footstool had to stop and rest at lunchtime, so we all sought shelter under an outcrop of shale that jutted out from the mountain's side. The footstool's timber creaked as he snored. The broom stared down at its frozen bristles in shock: they were filthy, matted, and beginning to fall out.

"We're taking too long," I complained, trying to leave space between my damp pages.

"I agree," the chamber pot replied.

"How are you going to convince the witch to turn us back?" I asked the chamber pot quietly. It was a terrible realisation: halfway to our destination, and I hadn't asked about the final step of the plan.

The chamber pot shrugged with his handle, and tucked himself deeper beneath the outcrop. "I'll appeal to her sense of morality," he said, "or whatever she has in its place. If that fails, I guess we'll have to kill her, and hope the curse comes undone that way."

"Woah," the broom interjected. "Kill? No one mentioned any killing before."

The chamber pot laughed, but there was an edge to it. "So, what will you do if she says no?"

The broom looked at the ground, but I was unperturbed.

"We'll figure something out, without needing to use violence."

"Sure," the chamber pot said, "you can go on believing that fairy tale, but if she turns you into a cockroach instead, then what?"

I leafed through my pages quickly, letting them cascade in front of the chamber pot's face in a show of confidence. The chamber pot didn't seem threatened.

He looked at me closely. "Can you see what's written inside you?"

"No, my eyes are on the cover."

"Huh. You're a book that can't even read itself. How useless."

"I've just about had enough of you," I hissed. "We're all taking a big risk trying to carry out your little adventure."

"And I can't stand any of you," the chamber pot replied bitterly. "You're all so helpless. A bunch of wishful-thinking victims. I've heard the master every night, and I've realised something that no one else has."

"What's that?"

"If I was once a man, then I was a violent one just like the master," the chamber pot said. "We all served him before we were turned into these freaks. If we were men, we were men like him."

"We were probably afraid of him, just like we are now."

24

"I'm not afraid of him," the chamber pot said. He saw the look on my cover. "I'm not. If we were men, we'd be the same size as him. We'd have two arms and two legs. That would change a lot of things."

We continued to climb a meandering path up the mountain, zigzagging under the wind, towards the destination that the chamber pot had seared into his mind.

Grey smoke drifted on the wind ahead of us as the footstool dragged himself through the thick deluge of snow. There was a small cottage ahead, tucked into the mountainside and surrounded by a thick crop of pine trees. The chamber pot egged us on towards it.

"That's the place," he said. "I think. Who else would live up here, besides a witch?"

The cottage was small, and made from piled timber. The roof was tilted at a sharp slope, encouraging the snow to fall down and away from the doorway. We arrived, and the footstool deposited us at the door, collapsing beside it. One of his legs had splintered away into a stub.

The chamber pot looked like he was trying to build up the courage to knock, so I beat him to it. I slammed my body heavily into the door twice, and then stood back. There was the sound of something being dropped, and the gasp of a woman.

"Get ready," the chamber pot said.

The door creaked open a little, and then suddenly Poubelle pushed it ajar with a mighty heave. She was draped in a tattered purple dress, and covered in furs and coats. Her hair was long and brown, her face was beautiful, and she was holding a crooked sickle in front of her with two trembling hands.

"Ha!" she yelled, making us jump.

Her eyes had been focused straight ahead, but when she looked down and saw us, she jumped back and screamed.

"Careful witch," the chamber pot said, crawling forward bravely. "No sudden movements, we have some things we'd like to discuss with you."

"You can talk?" she asked, backing into her cottage. "How can you talk?"

Emboldened by her reaction, we scraped and hopped over the door's threshold to confront her.

There was a bright flash, as brilliant as lightning, and suddenly I was on my back. I tried to pull myself up, but I was unable to move. I could see Poubelle above me grinning. Her cottage was small, and only furnished with a small brass sink, a bed, table, chamber pot, and a few chairs.

"Yes!" Poubelle sang, and raised her hands over her head in a victory dance. "It worked!"

"What have you done to us, witch?" the broom sobbed.

"Stop calling me that," Poubelle said, with a twitch in her eye. "I've paralysed you with a spell."

"Why?" the chamber pot demanded. "We're just here to talk with you."

"I've been preparing," she said with a loud giggle. "I figured he might have a few more tricks up his sleeve."

"Ma'am," I began, trying a gentler tactic. "We're here because you turned us into these miscellaneous items at the start of winter."

Poubelle looked thoughtful for a moment, and picked at something in her teeth with her sickle.

"No, I don't think I did," she said. "I've never even seen a spell like that before. Probably forbidden. My mother would've been able to tell you more about it, she was much better educated than me."

"Please, try to remember," I coaxed.

She thought for a moment, but then shrugged and knocked herself on the head with a knuckle. "Nope, sorry. Are you sure you've got the right person?"

"It must be you, Poubelle," the chamber pot said. "I've memorised your portrait from the castle. The master blames you for turning us into furniture."

Poubelle's face went a sudden shade of pale. "You came from the castle?" she asked.

"That's right."

"Your master, describe him for me?"

I opened my mouth to answer, but a long, dark shadow fell across the doorway. Poubelle screamed, and held her sickle up at the ready.

"Hello again," said the master with a grin.

Poubelle fell over backwards as she scrambled away from him. She pulled herself up on her table, but then slipped and crashed onto the ground.

"You!" she shouted.

"Yes, me. I had no idea you would be hiding from me on this very mountain. I was certain you'd have taken your chances crossing the tundra to a neighbouring kingdom." He bent down and poked his fingers into the tiny set of footprints we'd left in the snow. His eyes glanced away from Poubelle and landed on the footstool, tipped over and unable to move.

"Here are my runaways, and all in one convenient place too. Why are you lying on the ground?"

The master looked at the doorway thoughtfully for a moment. He backed away from the door, and disappeared for a moment. Poubelle glanced around the cabin, trembling. There was a shadow at the window near the brass sink, and then the master put his elbow through the glass. He climbed through the window frame.

"Trying to lure me through the doorway is a good trick," he said. "Your mother knew that one too."

"Don't you dare mention my mother," Poubelle spat. She pulled herself to her feet again.

The master kept his distance from the sickle that she held between them, choosing to sit himself comfortably on the sink's edge instead. Uncharacteristically, he'd bothered to get dressed. A thick leather boot kicked at the air, and he picked at the lint on his pantaloons and drawstring blouse.

"So, what now?" he asked, smiling devilishly. "Have you had sufficient time to consider my offer?"

"Curse you, and your offer," she answered.

"Your mother already tried that," the master said with a sigh, "and look where that got us."

He reached out to stroke her cheek, but she swung the sickle at him instead.

"Don't touch me Gervais," she said. "You must have the devil's luck if my mother wasn't able to kill you."

"Perhaps," he smiled. "Or, perhaps you underestimate me." He gestured towards us on the floor. "Do you like your mother's handiwork?"

"Her mother did this?" the chamber pot yelled.

"That's right," said Gervais, our master.

Poubelle glared at us with the most intense hatred I had

28

ever witnessed. It twisted her beautiful face into a cruel mask. The master had never hated any of us with such intensity.

"Do you want to break them?" Gervais asked. "Go ahead, I won't stop you. I've done it many times. It relieves a lot of tension."

"Yes, I'm sure you'd love me to turn my back to you for a moment," she said, redirecting her disgust back to him.

Gervais held up his hands in mock surrender. "Just trying to help, your highness."

"Highness?" I asked, feeling a growing sense of unease. "So, you're not a witch?"

"I'm the heiress to the castle that you've all been squatting in," Poubelle replied. She drew herself up taller, keeping her sickle carefully aimed at the master's heart. "I'll be the duchess soon, once winter ends and my people come looking for me."

"So, who is Gervais then?" the chamber pot asked.

"I don't like how talkative you've all become," the master said. "Don't forget that after I finish speaking with Poubelle, I'm planning to kill all of you for running away." He turned back to the duchess. "You're looking healthy. A few months living off the land has really kept the weight off."

She swung at him. The sickle sang through the air, but Gervais caught her wrist, and wrenched the blade from her. Poubelle yelled, clawing at his eyes, and trying to bite at the arm that held her. Gervais tossed the duchess back towards the table, and she landed on top of it. Plates and vegetables tumbled to the floor.

"Careful," the master said. "I have a nasty temper."

Poubelle held her wrist, which might have been broken. She looked up at Gervais, wide-eyed.

"What are you going to do?"

"The same thing I wanted to do at the start of winter," he said with a shrug. "I'm going to marry you, whether you want it or not, and become nobility."

"It takes more than marrying a duchess to become a noble," she shouted in disbelief. "The king will simply come and kill you, once he finds out what you did to my parents."

The master stopped. He tilted his head and squinted at her stupidly. "The king has to accept me, if I want to become a noble?"

Poubelle laughed, and pulled herself up onto a chair.

"Wait, are you being serious? You didn't know that?"

"Stop laughing," Gervais said, rising from the sink. "I hate it when you mock me."

"You thought you could kill my parents," she coughed, caught between laughter and anger, "force yourself on me, and that this country would just accept you?"

"The folks down in the village think I'll make a good duke," he spat, fists clenched. He gestured towards us. "My men weren't mercenaries, were they? They were your people. Your parents drove my own brother to starvation with their war taxes. Your own subjects wanted you dead!"

"And look at those subjects now," she said, pushing the table between Gervais and herself. "How far you've fallen! After you slunk into the castle, pretending to bring your harvests, you killed everyone I ever loved. I had to flee like a rodent. All winter, I've waited to hear the boots of your men coming up the mountain, but it's just you, isn't it? You're the only human left!"

"Your mother was a very creative sorceress," Gervais

admitted, stepping up onto the table to grab at her. "She knew how to transmute ten men at a time: turned their bodies to dust, and crammed their souls into any object she could see."

"Ha! Then she must have been reading a very strange spell book that evening." Poubelle was now squeezed between the table and the cottage wall. "Perhaps your men are fortunate. There were far worse spell books that she kept in her library. How did you survive?"

"I got lucky."

"You went in last, didn't you? You sent every other man into her chambers, before you poked your head in."

The master shrugged. "She ran out of objects to use in the bedroom. Last thing she did was cram my nephew's soul into the book she was carrying."

"So that's how you managed to kill her: you were a coward."

He was close to her now, leering over the table. Gervais held the sickle under her nose.

"You're coming back to the castle with me, and we'll talk this over. If the king's duke just so happened to have a terrible accident, but his daughter had already married, well...there's a chance."

"You know..." Poubelle leaned away from the blade, squaring her shoulders in the corner next to the table. "When a peasant wants to marry a duchess, the least he could do is prostrate himself."

She heaved upwards, and pushed over the table he was standing on.

The master's feet went out from under him, and he fell backwards on top of us. The footstool shattered, and the spirit of a baker screamed into the void. The master's elbow went into the chamber pot, and his head landed on me. The sickle skipped away from him, across the floor.

Poubelle was up and running for the dropped blade. The master screamed in pain, and then reached for the sickle that he'd dropped, which was just out of reach. The chamber pot must have drawn on a desperate strength that I lacked, because he tightened earnestly around the master's elbow, preventing him from straightening it and reaching the sickle.

Gervais reached out with his other arm instead, but Poubelle was already there. She grabbed the sickle, and swung it down at the master's chest. He tried to roll away, and the sickle sank into his shoulder, just above the collarbone.

She pulled the tool free with a spurt of blood, and tried to hit him again. The master lashed out with his foot and caught her in the stomach. Poubelle dropped the sickle, eyes bulging, and curled up in pain beside me. She gasped for air, desperately trying to fill her lungs. Her eyes were wet as she looked at me, and I tried to feebly fan her face with my pages.

Gervais tried to sit up, but the chamber pot still clung to him bravely. The master slammed his elbow into the ground, and the chamber pot shattered into pieces with a scream. His spirit looked like a grizzled bear-man as it evaporated. It suited him. Gervais pulled himself to his feet, using the sink to help. His white blouse was now crimson, and he had started sweating despite the cold. The arm below his shoulder wound swung limply.

Poubelle looked up at the panting, hairy master as he stood over us. Her hand lashed out and grabbed me.

"You never learned to read, did you Gervais?"

"Never needed to," the master said.

"This book is called: The Art of Binding Souls to Miscellaneous Objects."

She read a line of the book, an incantation of syllables, and then sniffed my pages deeply. I saw the sentences and diagrams lift from the paper and drift into her nostrils. Poubelle opened her eyes, and they shone blue and brilliant.

Gervais realised far too late what was happening. He swung the sickle at her head, but it fell limply from his crooked fingers. His body dissolved to dust and hair, and his soul was pulled, screaming, into Poubelle's hands. She held it there like a ball of flame while she clutched her stomach and gasped for air. She glanced around the room, looking for something to place the soul inside. The flames of Gervais' soul licked her skin, blackening her hands with heat. She looked at the sickle, and then thought better of it.

In the corner of her cottage, sat an old, stained chamber pot.

"Perfect," she said.

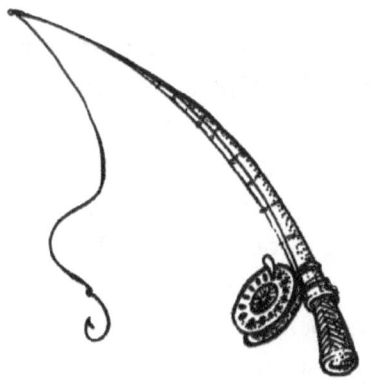

Wishing Fish

It was a Wednesday, the day that I met the wishing fish. I've forgotten a great many things in the past decades, but I distinctly remember it being a Wednesday. The lake rocked and bucked in the early morning wind as heavy droplets of winter rain cascaded across its surface in sheets, and pounded like ice against my neck. I hadn't eaten since yesterday, so I was miserable as usual.

My fishing line had sat undisturbed for the past half hour, and so I reclined in my canoe. My middle finger rested firmly against the nylon line of my bamboo rod, just above the hook keeper. For a brief moment I drifted off to sleep, but then I woke up, shaking my head roughly.

Empty crab traps sat at the front of my canoe. Holes had been torn in both of them, and the bait had been stolen. I rubbed my cold and sore shoulders. Fishing was no luxury for me: it was all I had to survive. I'd have to spend another long evening repairing the traps at the docks, instead of seeking shelter.

The fishing line was suddenly pulled taut. I managed to grab hold of the rod properly, just before it was pulled into the water. The tip of the rod bent away from me sharply, and as I glanced into the water, I saw a dark shape struggling to pull away from the canoe.

Instinctively, I spun myself around and anchored my feet so that the line wasn't caught under the canoe. The water frothed as the fish tried to break away. The canoe was pulled across the Sacred Lake, with me holding on and screaming as the fishing line zig-zagged desperately across the choppy water. The wake of the fish threatened to capsize me, until I felt the familiar sensation of the fish becoming exhausted.

With a few slow, careful turns of the reel handle, I pulled the catch beside the boat. The fish was enormous, close to the size of a tuna from the ocean. I reached for my net, and realised that it was far too flimsy to lift this creature from the water. The fish kicked and splashed, too tired to continue.

It turned to me, and breached the water.

"That really hurts," it said.

The chase had dug the fishing hook into the jaws of the fish, tearing a jagged line from the corner of its mouth.

"Sorry," I apologised. "It doesn't hurt as much if you just let me reel you in."

"I should've never eaten that worm," the fish said. "My

mother told me to avoid worms. There are folktales, you know. We tell stories about worms to our roe, to scare them."

"We all make mistakes," I replied, checking the long knife fastened to my belt. "I'm afraid I can't pull you up into the canoe without first goring you in the middle..."

The fish winced.

"Exactly. So, if you can manage to jump into the boat, that would actually help a great deal. I understand you must be somewhat exhausted, but it's what's best for the both of us. I could quickly cover your eyes and sever your spinal cord before you suffocate."

"I'd appreciate that a lot," said the fish. "You seem awfully calm at meeting a talking fish. Have you done this before?"

"Yes, just about every week," I said. "I've become quite used to all manner of talking sea life. There was a crab that promised to betray several other crabs to my traps if I let him go. I had a whiting the other day who begged me to let him mate before I ate him."

"Have you always been able to speak to fish?" it asked, submerging beneath the water again to get a better look at me.

I gestured to the fishing rod. It was handcrafted from red bamboo. "Ever since I bought this rod, I can hear you all in my head, clear as day."

"And you still eat us?" the fish asked.

"Yes, I do."

"I see," the fish said sadly. "I suppose bargaining with you is pointless then."

It swam away a short distance, turned, and leapt into the canoe. The canoe sunk deeper in the water. With my left hand, I covered the eye of the fish, and undid the clasp holding my knife.

"Oh, I just remembered something," the fish gasped. I took my hand away and splashed some water on its gills.

"Let me guess, you've suddenly remembered that you're magical?" I asked.

"You've heard that one before then?"

"Yes, you bet I have!" I shook my head and chuckled. "Just about every big fish I catch tries to offer me some sort of magic in exchange for their life. The first time I used this rod, I let the catch go free. However, it turns out that fish can't grant wishes. I mean, no offense, but you are just a fish."

It gurgled a sigh. "That's true, I am just a fish. I'm afraid I'm not magical at all. My teacher told us all just to say that as a last resort. I can't offer you any particular magic myself, but I do know about something that could help you."

This piqued my interest. I splashed some more water onto its gills.

"Tell me first, and then I'll see if it's worth letting you go. I have to eat, after all."

"There's an island," said the fish. "An island at the exact middle of this lake."

"I know it," I said. "It's more of a rock than an island, but go on."

"A few years ago, I spoke to an ancient armoured fish," it began. "At the time, it was dating my sister, so I think it was trying to impress me. I wasn't very keen on him though. The age gap was too significant."

"I'm hungry."

"So–" the fish continued quickly, "–he told me about something carved into the rock of that island. Something from a few hundred years ago, when he was a youth. There's a secret place there, from a forgotten race who lived here long before you did."

"What's in the secret place?" I asked.

"I wish I knew," said the fish. "But the way that he spoke about it, really arrogantly you see, made it sound like there was something incredible. A treasure that was sealed behind it."

"This is all pretty far-fetched," I said. "I don't particularly believe you, and as I said I'm pretty hungry."

"You can take me with you," said the fish hurriedly, "I don't mind sitting here in the boat. Just keep me breathing and you can eat me later if I turn out to be full of detritus."

I thought about it for a moment, as the fish lay gasping. Normally, my catch would have gone from negotiating, to pleading, to screaming abuse. But as I waited, it didn't offer anything else, and the idea of a treasure wasn't too much of a stretch. Very few people dared to even venture out onto the Sacred Lake. So, it was possible...

"Okay," I said, and gave the fish some more water across its body. "Let's see if there's anything there."

The rain was easing up when I spotted the small island in the centre of the lake. The fish had grown fidgety.

"Can you swim this thing faster please? I don't like being out here when the big birds wake up."

I left the hook in the fish's mouth, and pulled my blue tarp over so that a flying scavenger wouldn't spot it.

"Please hurry," begged the fish. "I'm drying out here."

"Where's this secret place supposed to be?" I asked, jumping out into the shallows, and pulling the canoe up onto the sand bar.

"You're looking for a large black rock," came the gasping voice from under the leather. "Just promise you'll come back quickly. If I'm telling the truth, come and release me."

"I'll be back quickly."

"Promise me."

"I promise," I said, feeling ridiculous.

The island was small. I could cross it from edge to edge in about forty paces. Small mud crabs scurried between the trunks of mangroves that grew from the mud. There was a small hill, made mostly of rock, that curled upwards at the centre of the island. The hill was carpeted in moss, and at its base was a round, black stone that had been hollowed out in the centre.

A thick fog had begun to settle across the island, preventing the dew from lifting. I heaved my feet through the mud and approached the stone, which was much older than the other rocks that littered the island. Its entire surface had been worn smooth by water currents. It stuck out so strangely, it must have been carried here on purpose, and hidden.

I looked through the hole in the centre of the stone, and wondered about the hidden treasure that the fish had spoken of.

What is it? I wondered to myself. *A horde of ancient gold? Riches, so I don't need to work again?*

I placed my hands on the stone and stuck my head through it. Nothing. I stood upright again.

"There has to be treasure here," I said to myself.

As soon as I had said it, the view through the hole shifted. A room appeared through the stone, filled with golden statues, chalices, and coins. I crawled through the hole easily, and found myself standing an ancient treasury, lit by flaming torches.

The hole in the stone was now a hole in the wall of this chamber. I looked closely, and saw that the hole was growing smaller each second. Far off in the distance, I could hear the wishing fish plead for its life.

"Where did you go?" came the faint voice through the hole.

I laid my coat on the ground of the treasury, and began piling gold on top.

"You promised!" came the desperate cry, but it was drowned out by the metallic clink of coins as I scooped them onto my coat.

The hole was still shrinking. I threw my coat, full to bursting, through the gap, and managed to squeeze through afterwards. I tumbled out onto the small island, and looked back as the picture of the treasury swirled and then vanished.

I returned to my canoe, with my coat slung over my shoulder and bursting with gold. When I arrived at the small canoe, however, I found that the fish had expired under the tarp. I didn't bother eating him. Instead, I left him on the island for the birds to find.

I wouldn't need to eat fish ever again.

* * *

A year later, I pulled the tarp off my canoe and pushed it into the water. I had grown several sizes larger. My head felt muddy, and my eyes stung each time I opened them. My shoulders were now permanently hunched from a lack of sleep.

My nightmares returned whenever I drifted off.

In my dreams, I saw the wishing fish watching me from the

island. His body was rotten and picked-apart by ibises. He kept screaming in agony.

The gold was nearly all spent, and my new friends with expensive tastes had vanished along with it. I realised, as the water lapped against the sides of the boat, that I missed the calm of fishing. I lay down in the canoe, watching the clouds roll in over the mountains. I cried silently for a time, and then I paddled to the island.

I couldn't find the body of the fish, and I don't know why I thought it would have been there in the first place. Perhaps I had wanted to apologise.

The stone sat resolute beneath the hill of the island. I stared into the hole and thought of the talking fish. I rubbed my eyes.

"I want peace," I whispered to the stone. The view on the other side showed an island that was covered in berry bushes, coconut palms, and pineapple shrubs. I crawled through.

The afternoon was wet, and the sun had been occluded by great clouds. I walked to the shore, but there was no boat on this island. The water was deep and blue. I looked for it across the horizon. In the haze, I couldn't even see a mainland.

A light rain began to fall, blown every which way by a gentle breeze. Birds cooed to each other from the thin trees that dotted the island. I returned to the stone, and saw that the hole was now gone. Instead, a new fishing rod leant against the basalt. I checked the line. It was strong.

I've now spent many years fishing from the shallows, and I no longer hear the fish speak to me when I catch them. When I do catch one, I pull the hook from its mouth and kiss it. Then I send it back into the water to swim again. Despite the gut-wrenching hunger I feel every day, as I scrounge for nuts and compete with the birds for seasonal fruits, I continue to fish, and I continue to set them free.

Perhaps this is my penance. Perhaps one day I'll catch the wishing fish again, and I'll be able to apologise for what I did.

The lake's water has become like glass these days. It is so still, that I can look down and see my own reflection clearly in the water's depths.

I sleep peacefully now.

The Glade

When Harry, Jim and Roza crested the hill, it was paradise. Nestled in a valley, the forest was a patchwork of red and green bamboo.

"How striking!" Roza exclaimed.

"That's pretty special isn't it, Harry?" Jim asked.

Harry nodded in awe. "It's the only species of red bamboo that's been discovered." He rubbed his eyes, "I'm not hallucinating, am I?"

"Just drink it all in," said Roza with a laugh, "who knows whether it'll be here for much longer." The group of friends grew silent for a moment, before Harry marched forward.

"Well, before the government lets the lumber companies

in, we might as well enjoy it." He began down the slope towards the forest, his enormous camping bag jangling behind him as he walked.

"You should have brought something smaller," Jim quipped. "A real man doesn't need much to go camping."

"A real man?" Harry said. "That's ridiculous. When your thimble of a backpack fails you, don't come begging me for toilet paper or something."

"Who needs toilet paper in a forest?" Jim said innocently. "That's what God made leaves for." He winked at Roza, but she gave him such a look of disdain that he dropped it and started whistling instead.

The bamboo began abruptly, like reaching the wall of an ancient fortress. When the other two had caught up to him, Harry was bent over and enthusiastically examining the floor of the forest. Small shoots of bamboo, like little palisades, grew up sharply at an angle from the edge of the forest.

"That's bizarre," said Harry. "The forest, by all means, should be growing up and out of this valley. It stops so abruptly."

"Perhaps the soil is toxic over here?" suggested Roza.

Harry nodded, "that's possible. Still, you'd expect some dithering of the terrain."

"Save the mystery and deduction for the red bamboo you two," Jim chipped in. "That's the real excitement right there."

"It's much farther in," Roza added. "I'd venture we'll have to spend a night in the forest."

Despite the foliage being dense and difficult, they made decent progress. Harry, who worked as a lab biologist, was excited whenever he spotted any local wildlife.

"Thanks for inviting me on this trip Jim," he said. "It's nice to get out once in a while."

"Of course," Jim replied. "It's for old times' sake. I've wanted to visit for a long time. It's been eating at me. Besides, it'd be a shame to come without you both."

"I'm a bit confused about why you invited me though," said Roza. "We weren't particularly close in high school."

Jim poked at his forehead. A large black blister jutted out from the skin. "Well, I tried getting in contact with some of my close friends from the glory days. Some don't answer anymore."

Harry winced, and landed a strong hand on Jim's shoulder.

"Well, *we* appreciate the invite. People change their numbers and forget about the past. It's nice that you thought of us."

They journeyed deeper into the forest, and Jim whistled some more. For the first hour or so, no creature revealed itself. Roza would stop every thirty minutes or so in order to photograph their progress. As they ventured deeper, Harry had to occasionally brandish his machete against particularly thick pockets of the foliage.

The sun was no longer clearly visible. Instead, it was sifted a hundred times through the small green leaves above. The light and shadows shifted in a beautiful dance as a distant wind stirred the canopy overhead.

It was while their heads were locked upwards, mesmerised by the foliage above them, that they heard the sound of something snapping ahead. The ground moved suddenly beneath them, throwing Jim off his feet. Lying prone on his back, he saw the immense shadow roll forward and topple the surrounding bamboo like matchsticks.

Two enormous black claws, covered in fur, engulfed the canopy ahead of them, and tore the bamboo from the earth with another tremor that managed to throw Harry and Roza to the ground as well. As the three of them lay cowering in the spray of earth that fell from the swathe of unearthed forest, a gargantuan head appeared above them.

Its fur was black with a bold orange crescent across its neck and chest. Its teeth were like a dog's. Two lidded eyes of black sat either side of its snout.

"Oh, hullo there," it said.

Between its lips were long straws of thin foliage that it sucked on, and yet the sun bear somehow managed to speak around the food.

Roza clutched her heart and began to laugh nervously. Jim lay prone, his eyes wide and frantic, focused on the creature's paws. They sat in silence for a moment before Jim began to make a gurgling sound in the back of his throat that threatened to turn into a scream.

"Hello," Harry said quickly, afraid that Jim would anger it. "I'm sorry, I didn't know that...you...talking creatures lived here."

The bear approximated a smile as best it could, and held out the smallest finger of its claw. It took Harry a moment to realise he should grab it. The finger lifted him up to his feet effortlessly, and then assisted Roza in standing up. As it approached Jim, he quickly scrambled to his feet instead of accepting the help.

"You look familiar somehow," said Jim.

Roza's heart was aflutter. "I've never seen anything like

you."

"Well," said the sun bear in a deep voice like chocolate, "I usually try to avoid meeting humans whenever I can. Perhaps I'm getting rusty."

He stood on his hind legs, and with his mammoth height he looked out over the forest's canopy easily. The sky was pink and orange behind him.

"It's going to get cold soon," the bear said. "Come with me."

Harry looked back at Roza, who was wide-eyed with wonder. Her gaze didn't leave the bear for a moment, as she followed him dutifully into the darkness. Jim was shaking his head.

"I'm going with Roza," Harry said softly. "A talking creature like this? Whoever heard of such a thing?"

"No one, probably," Jim replied under his breath. "Because he probably ate them before they could tell anyone else."

"Actually," said the bear from a great distance ahead. "I only really eat honey, fruit, and insects. In the bear family, you might as well consider me to be a vegetarian."

Roza made a cooing sound in her throat. "Me too!"

"How lovely," replied the bear. "We must be kindred spirits."

It led them slightly away from their intended path towards the red bamboo. Instead, they made camp in a small glade that the bear had recently cleared. The dirt was still churned underfoot from its excavations. The meal that they shared was relatively uneventful. The bear prepared them a chilled, spicy soup with leeks and fermented shoots. They sat upon furniture that the sun bear had quickly fashioned from bamboo for them. Roza spoke to it about birdhouses in her hometown, and after some discussion and drawings in the mud, the bear was able to fashion several small dwellings for a species of blue lyre that happily sang for them just as the sun finally set. When the evening sky began to drizzle in the dead of the night, the enormous bear wove the canopy above them carefully to prevent the deluge from reaching them.

Harry slept peacefully on a bed of leaves and loam, except for when he was awoken by Jim's tossing and turning, or Roza's hissed laughter as she conversed with the bear all night.

By morning, Jim was tugging at their sleeves like a toddler and begging to go. His blister seemed to be aggravating him again. He kept rubbing it distractedly.

"Come on, let's go see that red bamboo and then book it," he said.

"Please enjoy the forest," the bear said. "Oh, but I must inform you about the rules here. Please be careful not to disturb the balance of life. If you must take something from the creatures or the plants here, make sure that you replace it quickly. I'll come and find you tomorrow to check that you are respecting the forest."

"Of course!" said Roza with a beam. "I can't wait to see you again."

"We'll make sure to pay our respects," Harry answered, and kicked Jim.

"Yeah will do," said Jim, without lifting his gaze to meet the beady eyes above him.

"Make sure you do Jim," it said with a warm smile.

Once they had been walking for an hour or so south,

towards the patches of red bamboo on the horizon, Jim spoke up again.

"No way in hell am I going back to see that thing," he said loudly.

Harry and Roza followed behind Jim as he forged a path ahead, and glanced at each other.

"I'm not going back," he repeated. There was defiance in his eyes. A challenge to stop him.

"If that's what you want," said Roza. "Oh, damn. I should have asked him about the red bamboo. He'd probably know something about it. Why didn't I think of that earlier?"

"We were tired," Harry said. "We're *all* still tired," he continued, eyeing Jim.

The trio paused as a cry rang out from the forest. It was an animalistic scream, to their left. Roza immediately took off towards the sound. Harry followed.

Jim stayed firmly where he was.

"Hey guys, don't go running off and getting lost!" Jim's shouts echoed from behind them, but Roza was already rushing through the forest to find the source of the cries.

In a clearing ahead, a bearded monkey lay at the bottom of a rocky outcrop. Its leg was twisted backwards behind its spine, and it mewled pitifully. From its vantage point above, a dull, malnourished tiger watched the monkey scream. Its tail swished behind it in a fluid motion, somewhat carelessly, as it descended towards the screams. Roza broke into the clearing. The tiger froze for a moment, but then dashed for the wounded monkey to snatch it away.

Roza pulled off her right hiking boot and hurled it with the assurance of the Women's College softball captain. It struck the adolescent tiger on its side, causing the animal to change course rapidly and flee into the darkness of the bamboo again.

Roza dashed to the monkey, and swaddled it in her jacket. Harry burst onto the scene, huffing, and looked down at the bundle.

"You sure that's a good idea?" he asked, looking around. "We promised to repay anything we take. I don't know what the exchange value for a red-shanked douc is."

"What's a douc?" Roza asked.

"That's the name of the monkey."

"Well, I'm not going to take it home with me," Roza said curtly. She scratched it under the chin. "I'm just going to escort it to the sun bear for safe-keeping. He'll know how to treat it."

"I suppose," said Harry. "As long as you're willing to take care of it."

Roza sat the douc in her backpack so it could see behind her, and gently placed the flap of her bag on its head for safety. "I only have to take care of it for a day or so."

They returned to Jim, who was waiting for them while he picked at his forehead. He breathed a sigh of relief. "Thought I'd lost you both."

"No such luck," said Harry. He winced as Jim's fingers came away bloodied.

"For heaven's sake stop touching it," said Roza. She sat her pack down, handed the douc to Harry, and dug around for the first aid kit. After some liberal application of betadine, Jim's face looked a lot worse, but he was smiling now instead.

"Hey wow," he said. "It doesn't itch as much now."

"Let me know if you need some more," she said.

The rest of the day continued without much interruption. They paused to take pictures of a small brook, where a bright blue pheasant bathed.

"This place is so untouched," Harry remarked.

They walked for most of the day, stopping occasionally for a food break. By midday they had reached the red bamboo. For all of their anticipation, the sight greeted them abruptly. The stalks of bamboo were much taller than the surrounding species. They grew a good forty metres into the air.

Harry wiped the sweat from his forehead. The day had grown humid in the valley. They dropped their packs, except for Roza, who placed it carefully on the ground. The small douc had been whimpering a lot during the journey. Each step that she had taken caused a small pearl of agony to escape its throat.

"Rest now," she said, and gave it some water from her canteen.

Harry stood amazed at the height of the culms as they pierced the sky. The leaves were a deep burgundy. He took a small knife and scraped at one branch. The flesh came away red and then white.

"They haven't been stained," he said to no one in particular, but jumped when Jim spoke beside him.

"Must be some sort of mutation."

"I suppose so," Harry began, but then looked around at the surrounding forest. "But why in such small clusters? And why so far apart? I can't see any other clusters nearby. There must be a good three hundred metres between each pocket of red bamboo."

"Animals sometimes carry the seeds of plants," Roza said

simply, as she returned from her scout around the cluster.

"I guess so," said Harry. "That's the troubling thing though. If it was transported by animals, you'd see a much wider spread. If this species exhibits some sort of mass flowering, then we should see the seeds spread throughout the forest much more liberally. However, they're just contained to this small glade in the centre of the forest."

"How long do you think they'd take to germinate?" Roza asked.

"I've heard it takes some bamboo a hundred years to sprout seeds," Harry said sadly. "It's a shame. I'd love to take a sample home with me."

"Well," said Roza, holding up a handful of something that looked like pine nuts. "I found a branch all the way back there that's spewing seeds."

Harry breathed in deeply for a moment, and then plucked the seeds out of Roza's hands. "I don't believe it!" He said with a shout. "What are the chances? Bamboo usually flowers at a similar time, I wonder why this one hasn't sprouted yet?"

"I don't think we should take them," Jim said. "How long should it take to flower, did you say? A hundred years? The bear won't let you walk out with something that valuable."

Harry shrugged. "He might."

Jim slapped his forehead repeatedly. "What will he want in return for it?"

"Woah, what's wrong champ?" Harry asked.

"There's something that's been bothering me, it's on the tip of my tongue."

"Are you unwell?" Roza asked, threatening to dig around in the first-aid kit again.

"I just feel like this is all really familiar," Jim replied. "It's like I've had a dream about this happening, but I can't remember how it ends."

The earth shook. The suddenness of it caused the seeds that Harry had been holding to be scattered across the ground.

"It's coming for us," yelled Jim, wide-eyed.

"Calm down," reasoned Roza, who was trying to stand as the ground gave way again.

Harry, on his hands and knees, saw a single seed between his knees. He picked it up, and slipped it into his pocket just as the bear barrelled into the glade with a hearty welcome. The ground stopped shaking.

"Friends," said the bear as it stood uneasily on its hind legs to reach its full height. "How have you enjoyed my forest?"

"It's been wonderful, sir," said Roza, starry-eyed once more.

"Has it now?" said the bear with a smile. His eyes drifted towards the backpack that contained the crying douc. "What do we have here?"

"I saved it," said Roza giddily. She opened her bag and unwrapped the creature from her jacket. She lifted the small monkey up to the gargantuan bear, who sat puzzled.

"I see, my child," said the bear sadly. "You saved it did you?"

"Yes," Roza said with a smile.

The bear held out an enormous paw, and Roza placed the douc into its palm.

"There, there," said the bear. "You've had a difficult journey, haven't you?"

The douc sat placidly, staring up at the sun bear in perfect stillness. It had stopped making noises, and it was only then, in that silence, that Roza realised how much it had sobbed in her backpack.

The bear delicately wrapped its other hand around the head of the douc, and broke its neck with a loud snap. It threw the body of the douc into the darkness of the bamboo, where a patient tiger grabbed the monkey by its throat and happily dragged it away.

Roza let out a scream and fell to the ground, shaking. "Why?" she begged.

"My dear," said the bear. "Did you really think you were helping that poor creature? Each step you took was agony for it. You also stole that tiger's meal for the day. What you did wasn't humane."

The bear paused and made a face of disgust.

"Ugh, humane. Even the word contains the word 'human'. You need to understand, Roza, being humane doesn't translate to nature. You shouldn't have interfered."

"But you're a vegetarian," she said. "A kindred spirit."

"Indeed," said the bear. "I wouldn't ever eat the douc. However, you assumed that because you hated eating animals, the tiger was wrong for doing what was simply natural to him. Your charity, even well-intentioned as it was, is still interference with the laws of Gaia. The douc would've rather died than go on in the agony that you provided. Here, let me just show you."

The sun bear of the bamboo forest reached down delicately once again, but this time it's great fingers gently touched Roza's leg. Then, with the force of a pneumatic press, the bear squeezed and pulverised everything below Roza's knee. Her screams echoed through the glade, frightening the nearby wildlife. Even the tiger, eating the douc upon a rock, paused to listen.

Roza clutched her heart. Her fingernails desperately dug into her left breast, willing her heart to keep beating, hoping that the pain her fingers were inflicting would drown out the pure, silver pain that froze her spine and burned in her chest.

Harry ran towards Roza and tried to drag her away. He grabbed her right arm and pulled, but her leg was dragged across the ground like liquid.

"Stop," she pleaded in a faint whisper, and then she screamed. Harry dropped her again, and staggered backwards.

The bear smiled down at him. "Was there anything you found in my forest that you took?" he asked. The long, stalactite teeth of the bear were suddenly no longer friendly. "I think I can smell something on you that belongs to me."

Harry willed himself to run, but a sharp pain near his pocket was crippling him.

"Jim was quite right," said the bear. Jim had fallen face-down on the loamy floor of the forest, he was weeping.

"Animals do indeed carry this particular seed of bamboo: a species of rodent called human."

Harry willed himself to move. The left side of his body couldn't move properly. He hobbled away from the bear with his good arm and leg.

Am I having a stroke? Harry thought, as he cut his elbow on the forest floor beneath him. His face hit the dirt and he tasted some of it. His leg kept kicking reflexively, pushing his face further into the dirt as he struggled to ascend the small incline.

Something sharp pierced him between his neck and collarbone, and the pain forced him up out of the dirt again. There was a loud snapping noise, and Roza's screams stopped abruptly. Harry turned to see the bear finish breaking Roza's neck. It tossed her body into the darkness beyond the glade, where the tiger was waiting.

The bear bent over Jim, and cooed as it stroked his back. From where he was lying, Harry saw Jim arch over backwards in pain. The enormous blister on his forehead burst with brown blood, and he collapsed on the floor.

"Not again!" he screamed.

The bear's deep and chocolate voice boomed. "I see your memory is back to normal. Thank you for listening to the spell, and returning to pay your debts."

"What debts?" Harry asked, groggily.

"Let's see," the bear said thoughtfully. "He stole an entire seed pod, which is worth a hundred years of life in the forest. The two friends who were with you then, had a combined lifespan of 50 years between them. Then your friend Roza here is twenty-something as well. Since Harry will soon become part of the forest as well, I'm willing to round it up, and say that your debt here is complete."

The bear picked Jim up like a doll, collected his tiny pack, and carried him back the way they had come. "The balance of the forest has been returned."

Harry tasted blood, and was having difficulty breathing. His leg kicked without him controlling it.

Stop it, he thought feebly, but his leg had no feeling anymore.

Something pierced him in the chin, and he turned his face

away from the pain. A razor-thin shoot of red bamboo grew mightily out of his neck, and up into the sky above him. Harry looked down to see one leg was twisting downwards into the soil like a root. It snapped and then curled, wrapping around and around itself as it drilled into the rock, soft clay, and dirt below him.

He looked up at the sky, and could only see from one eye, as the other was now skewered on another shoot of red bamboo. He watched that eye as it dutifully rose up, up, up into the air.

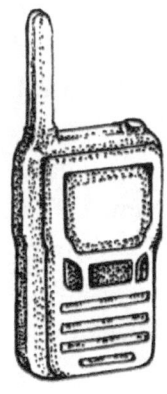

Pacific

A thousand birds circled in the air above the coastline, heralding a dark omen. Colonel Mustav watched them from the passenger seat. His body was now cocooned in a chlorine-drenched hazmat suit, and he was sweating uncontrollably. As the military truck approached the beach proper, the only sound Mustav could hear was the deep rasping of his own breath. The smell of chlorine and sweat was making him even more nauseous than the morning's briefing had. Surely, the hairs of his nose must have been eroded from the stench by now.

The driver swung the truck wide, and they stopped just before the waterfront. The Colonel kicked his door open, and was saluted by Captain Harker as he disembarked from the truck. Mustav returned the salute, as best as the hazmat suit would allow. Captain Harker, despite also wearing the bright yellow getup, was grinning uncontrollably.

"Status report, Captain?" Mustav asked.

"All clear, Colonel," replied the Captain. He gestured towards the water, and the Colonel waddled in that direction, flanked by two enlisted men. "We've cordoned off the area, and have issued general warnings across the radio and television services, warning residents to leave the area." He pointed to the early-warning tsunami sirens mounted atop the beach club to their left. "We're using the broadcast to send a warning on loop."

They arrived at the boardwalk, and the ocean stretched out beyond them. That was when the Colonel saw the creature. It was the size of a seven-storey building, and had beached itself on the sand.

"Estimate of contact?"

"It's biological, Colonel. Currently non-threatening. Civilian specialists are examining it. Contact precautions. Snipers in position."

They squelched and huffed their way across the sand towards it. The Captain indicated a safe distance for the Colonel, and then jogged the rest of the way to the mass. About thirty figures in yellow milled about it. There was a science team positioned precariously close to the underside of the mass, taking samples.

The Colonel waited. The Captain came jogging back with another figure in tow. Marine birds buzzed about, landing atop the blight, and trying to tear pieces of it away. The creature was a greenish-brown, and had a large, armoured head. Approximately halfway along its body, the armour became wetter and softer, terminating in a small tail, like a tadpole.

"This is Dr Jones, biologist." The Captain was still preppy and excited. Dr Jones was the opposite. The middle-aged woman gave the Colonel a withering look and removed her hazmat helmet.

"Ma'am, refasten your helmet please," the Captain said, dropping his smile.

"No need to," Dr Jones said lethargically. She unzipped the hazmat suit to her navel, and fished around inside her jacket pocket. She produced a cigarette, and promptly lit one.

"Ma'am, I'll ask you again to obey contact precautions."

The enlisted men either side of Mustav shifted their weight, uncertain.

"We have snipers at the ready," Mustav said, cutting to the chase. "I need to know if the contact is dangerous or not."

"It's definitely dangerous," she said, and took a long, slow drag from her cigarette.

The Captain turned away and began issuing orders through his radio at the men stationed on rooftops.

"Do you have a hypothesis?" Colonel Mustav asked. "Could it be a bio-weapon?"

"I'm not certain about that," Dr Jones said. "We'll need to have a team come in and remove it. It's going to destroy the surrounding hundred kilometres of coastline."

"Prepare to engage," Colonel Mustav commanded the Captain sharply. "Prep the artillery. Request air support."

Dr Jones frowned and shook her head. "Sorry, Colonel,

that won't be necessary. I assumed you would have recognised what it was from here."

Mustav stared at her, and then back at the mass. It did look familiar, but he couldn't place it.

"What the devil is it?" he asked.

"It's a turd," she replied simply. "It's the biggest piece of crap I've ever seen."

The Colonel looked at the mass floating in the water, the size of the building. He paused, estimating the scale of the creature that could create it. Then, he unfastened his hazmat helmet, and breathed in the distinct smell of faeces on the wind.

There was a long pause as each person admired it there on the sand. The Colonel accepted Dr Jones' second offer of a cigarette.

"I need to call my superiors."

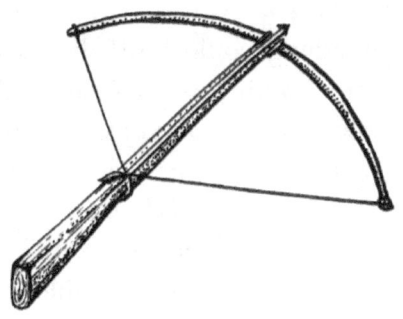

Little Red

The sun had nearly set by the time Grandma called me inside from chopping wood. The axe she had given me was far too large, but it was apparently a gift from a lumberjack many years ago. My 12-year-old arms shook beneath its weight as I heaved it down one final time. The log of wood didn't just split beneath its swing: it shattered. I left the axe buried in the cutting stump, scooped up the shards of wood, and skipped inside the small cottage that I shared with Grandma. After wiping my feet on the backdoor mat, I dusted the splinters and wood chips off my dress.

Grandma was in the kitchen baking. She had a sweet-tooth, which explained the large, canine-like dentures that she left on her bedside table each night. She heard me as I tip-toed up behind her, as quietly as I could. Grandma could always hear me.

She pointed to the pantry next to the oven.

"Fetch me something would you?" she asked.

This had become routine for us. Grandma's knees would creak when she stood, and the air left her lungs in a deep gasp whenever she sat down. Anything that required too much movement was now my responsibility.

"It's in the back. Blue box, bottom shelf."

I dropped the wood on the kitchen table, and pulled open the heavy oak door of the pantry. Various cured meats and strings of garlic hung from the roof. Seasonal fruits and vegetables were carefully arranged along the shelves, perfuming the air. I crouched low in the small space, and pushed aside an enormous mason jar of sugar. In the very back corner of the shelf I could see a wooden box, which had been painted blue an eternity ago. It was rectangular, and clasped at the front.

I brought it out into the kitchen, and placed it on the table carefully. Grandma withdrew a ladle of sugary concoction, which simmered atop the wood-fuelled stove. She slurped from the ladle greedily.

Grandma was hairy for a woman. I brought it up once, and she had complained that her own mother was too friendly with a bushy sailor, whatever that meant.

"You can open it, my dear," she said, watching me through enormous spectacles. "It's a present if you can learn how to use it."

The latch at the front should have rotated, but it took

some prying before I could force the rusted mechanism to move. It gave way with a creak. Inside, there was an ancient device, shaped like the crucifix atop our town's chapel. There were also some short arrows, and a jar filled with some putrid liquid. I pulled the wooden device from the box, and held its sturdy weight with both hands.

"What is it?" I asked, slightly annoyed that it wasn't a toy, or a more manageable axe.

"A tool from your Nonna's trade," she replied, and took the device from me. "That was a very long time ago, mind you, but it should still work."

She opened the glass jar with a grunt, and dipped her fingers into the brown fluid, fishing. She pulled out a long, fibrous chord, dripping with oil, and strung it to the device with practised ease. I now recognised the contraption from my history textbook, and squealed with glee.

"It's a real crossbow!"

"Yes, but please call it a balestra for my sake," Grandma said. She snapped her fingers, and the fire on the stove extinguished. Then, she picked up the iron-tipped arrows from the box, and ushered me outside.

I did a cartwheel out the backdoor, followed by Grandma. "Keep your back straighter, my dear!" she called. "Otherwise you'll lose your balance on poor terrain."

Grandma easily lifted the wood axe in her right hand, and took the blade to the broad Eucalyptus tree that stood in the middle of our garden. With two confident swings, Grandma carved a bold 'X' into the trunk of the tree, before returning the axe to the stump in the yard. I giggled with excitement.

"Do you remember the dance moves I taught you?" she

asked.

I furrowed my eyebrows. "The one for the family dance-off last year? Or the one you do when you've had too much drink?"

"The first one, my dear," Grandma blushed. "Don't ever do the second one. Ahem. Not until you're married anyway." She stood firmly between me and the target. "First position, please."

By reflex, I turned and stood at a 90-degree angle, with my dominant leg facing away from her.

"Good, good." Grandma notched a bolt into the crossbow and pulled it back so that it was loaded. "Next position."

I held my left hand up, elbow pressed tightly against my body. My palm was flat and slightly cupped. I blew her a kiss.

"Perfect," she said, and placed the balestra's grip in my free hand. "Step three."

I heaved the contraption up and onto my left palm. It was bulky, but felt light compared to the flour that Grandma made me haul from the grocer's truck each month. The grip felt familiar, and I realised it had been carved into the same shape as the handle on Grandma's axe.

"Next," came the call.

I winked with my non-dominant eye, and tilted my head to the side. My cheek connected to the shaft of the balestra, and I could see clearly down the length of the contraption, facing the X.

"That's called welding your cheek," Grandma explained.

I nodded, now the dance made sense. Grandma had a habit of doing this sort of thing. For a full year, she'd made me dust the cottage with a rope binding my upper arms to my torso.

The next month I won the district's fencing championship.

"Aim slightly higher than you think you should," Grandma instructed. "Squeeze the release gently now. No hurry."

I held my breath, and pulled the trigger under the grip.

Holding one's breath is an important part of the dance routine, Grandma had said.

The bolt flew from the balestra, and sank with a satisfying *thunk* into the wood of the tree. The bolt landed a few centimetres above the X.

"I missed the bullseye!" I complained, stomping my foot.

"Yes, you did," said Grandma. Her face betrayed no emotion. "Try it again."

I practised until the fading light made it too difficult to continue. Grandma stacked some of the chopped wood into the boiler and sent me inside to bathe.

Later that night, when Grandma tucked me into bed, she placed the blue box under my bed.

"Practise every day," she said.

"I promise Grandma."

She sat down slowly in the rocking chair by my bed.

I always felt safe when Grandma was in her rocking chair. If I suddenly woke up in the middle of the night, she would always be there: awake and ready to comfort me in the darkness. The night grew colder, and a howling wind tore at our small cottage. Grandma her favourite red shawl tucked around her legs to keep her warm. Something scurried across the roof. Its feet scratched at the corrugated steel.

"Tell me a story Grandma?" I asked.

"Very well, my dear," she whispered. Her chair creaked in

a reassuring rhythm that never failed to send me to sleep. "Which story would you like to hear?"

"The one about the young girl and the wolf."

"That one again?" her voice sounded annoyed, but even in the faint moonlight, I could see a smile grow beneath her grey eyes. "There once was a girl, just like you, who lived with her Nonna."

I rolled over in my bed, and fell asleep before Grandma had begun describing the wolf.

* * *

I was startled awake by a tapping sound against the glass windowpane above my bed. The night was still, and as I looked up, I saw a long, skeletal finger tentatively poke the glass.

"Grandma!" I said with a gasp. The rocking chair was empty.

The finger tapped again at the glass.

Tap, tap, tap.

I closed my eyes tightly, even though Grandma told me that it was a very poor survival reflex. I opened them again, and the finger was gone.

Grandma appeared at my door, and sat back in her rocking chair once again with a deep sigh. The chair rocked rhythmically, and I felt my eyelids grow heavy once more.

"What was that thing outside Grandma?" I asked.

Grandma was silent for a long time, watching the place where the long finger had caressed and assessed the glass.

"Just a tree tapping against the window, my dear. It's nothing to be afraid of. Go to sleep."

I jumped awake once more when a deep moaning came

from outside. The wind was now still. Grandma's rocking chair was empty again, so I reached under my bed for the blue box. I laid it on my bed, and opened it. The balestra was still inside. I closed the box, and placed it under my downy pillow. I looked up at the roof, and tried to study the broken plaster there.

Grandma appeared at my door once again. She looked tired, and had to catch her breath before she had the courage to sit again. Her knees and elbows cracked and popped, until she finally collapsed into the chair.

"Why are you awake, my dear?" she whispered.

"What was that noise Grandma? It sounded like some poor animal howling."

"That's just a guardian keeping vigil outside. It's nothing to be afraid of, my dear. Go to sleep."

I pouted a little. "Are you going to leave me again Grandma? I can't sleep properly if you do."

"Very well," she said. "I won't leave again."

She sang me to sleep in a forgotten language.

I awoke for the last time that night, as a deep thrumming filled the air. I could hear the sound of sick and hollow drums pounding. Grandma sat still in her rocking chair. Her head was turned like an owl's, searching all around and behind her.

"What's that noise Grandma?" I asked.

Her neck pivoted sharply, and her eyes locked onto me. Her face was white and expressionless.

"Oh," she said. "That's just the local marching band practicing for the parade."

"There's no parade this month, Grandma."

"Damn these legs." It took all of Grandma's strength to

stand. Her arms and legs shook with the effort.

"Should I be afraid, Grandma?" I asked.

"Yes," she said. "It's time to be afraid."

I sat up in bed, and pulled the balestra out from its box with trembling hands.

"I'm going to have to take care of this one, my dear," she said.

In the moonlight, I saw Grandma's body crack in half.

Her skin and nightdress ripped, and her ribs stuck out from the wound like the large, white teeth of a whale. Her head bent down and under her legs. I screamed, but the thing that Grandma had become ignored me. Little red fibres from her shawl spread out across the floor underneath her, and she was carried off, down the stairs and into the darkness.

I sat, petrified.

Downstairs, I could hear furniture being tossed. A deep reverberating roar filled the air.

Grandma's lessons on meditative breathing came back to me, and I forced myself to breathe slowly and evenly, even while my heart pounded, and my skin surged with pins and needles. I waited until my hands stopped shaking, then I cocked a bolt against the balestra's string. Withdrawing another bolt, I placed it between my teeth, the same way that Grandma held her spare clothes pegs.

I crept down the length of the hallway, and down the stairs. After years of trying to creep up on Grandma, my feet were now silent and certain. I could sense the air abuzz with energy. We'd always lived far away from the flow of electricity. Grandma said the TV dulled your senses, and electric lights weakened your eyes.

I arrived at the bottom of the stairs, and peered around the corner to check the kitchen. The table and chairs had been shoved to the edges of the room, as though a current had torn through the centre of the kitchen. I slunk from shadow to shadow, making my way towards the front yard, where I felt the source of the energy surging.

A different sound filled the air, and it chilled my spine. It sounded like the voices of little children: laughing and screaming in delight. I arrived at the back door in a crouch, and turned the knob slowly. Then, I threw the door open and jumped back. My right foot planted itself automatically behind me. I raised my left palm, lifted the balestra, winked and welded my cheek to the comb of the weapon.

Outside, a hulking creature clawed its way towards the house. It screamed in the voice of drums and a hundred toddlers. The creature that Grandma had become was biting at it, tearing away the flesh at its side as the intruder tried to scale our small picket fence.

"The wolf spirit," I whispered under my breath.

The head of the creature snapped up. It had no eyes, but its two long ears swivelled in my direction. It was just like how Grandma had described it. A large gash had been torn along the side of the beast, but it showed no signs of stopping.

Run. The command came from the wet puckering maw of Grandma.

Instead, I held my breath, and squeezed the balestra's trigger firmly. The bolt flew straight, and buried itself into the snout of the spirit. It reeled away, and ducked under the cover of the fence. I notched another bolt.

The spirit leapt up and over the fence, and grabbed at

73

Grandma with one of its filthy, monkey-like hands. It collected a fistful of her red tendrils, and pulled violently. Grandma screamed as the long, red strands of her spirit body were torn out from inside her. Grandma hit the ground, and the wolf's teeth sank into her. It shook its head, and Grandma was a blur in front of my balestra.

I aimed my second shot, and waited.

The wolf finished shaking Grandma, and tossed her to the side as it charged at me.

I waited. I waited until its mouth was open and nearly around me. I waited until I could smell the decay on its breath, and saw the blood on the tips of its teeth, and then I fired. The bolt sank into the back of the spirit's throat, and a plasm gushed from the wound.

Its hands went to the back of its mouth to try and pull the dart free, which is when I ran. Behind me, the voice of a hundred children begged me to come back. I tore around the side of the house and past the old Eucalyptus tree.

The wolf spirit was behind me. I felt its breath on the back of my neck. I hurled the balestra to the left, and then dove towards the tree stump. My hands wrapped around the axe handle, and I pried the weapon free of the stump, just as I felt the icy grip of the wolf's hand wrap around my ankle. I swung blindly, which Grandma would have been dismayed to see.

The axe connected with the creature's temple, lodging there for a moment, before I managed to pry it loose. It was a movement that felt sloppy. My hands must have been shaking. The spirit collapsed to the ground, and I sank the axe head between its eyes to finish the job.

In the cold dawn air, there was the sound of a baby

screaming, but I ignored it. I pulled the axe free as though I were once again chopping wood. I centred myself, and then swung down again. When I pulled the axe head free this time, the sounds of children had stopped.

I dropped the axe.

When I found Grandma, she was crumpled on the grass. I turned her over, and she rolled like a bag of bones. I didn't sense any life from the maw that came from her middle. Now that her nightdress was torn, I could see rows of beady black eyes that surrounded the mouth. I couldn't find her head.

Even though the grass was covered in dew, I sat beside Grandma. I tried to cry, but instead I just felt numb. Grandma had a favourite song. I couldn't remember the words, so I just hummed the tune for her. Then I buried Grandma's body in the deep grave we'd dug a year ago.

Just in case, Grandma had said, when we'd dug it.

I finished patting the earth down by the time the sun had risen. That's when I found my tears.

In my room, Grandma had left a travel suitcase. She'd packed it months ago, full of spare clothes and other necessities. On the front of the suitcase, written in her careful cursive, there was a street address. I took the keys to our old Mitsubishi from the kitchen counter, and packed some bread for the journey.

Outside, Grandma's old car spluttered to life, and I backed it out across the grass.

I allowed myself a moment to look at our cottage in the rear-view mirror. It was lit brightly in the morning sun, and the chickens were clucking as they waited to be let out of the roost.

"Goodbye," I whispered, and reached down with my foot to try and find the accelerator.

CEO

Timur was a strange employer, but then again, I'd only known him for a week. He'd thrown a welcome-to-the-business luncheon on Friday, and I'd gravitated towards him immediately. It was only polite to meet with him first, but even if the circumstances hadn't dictated it, I would have wanted to speak with Timur. There was an unmistakable grace to his movements. He was strange, yes, but he held your gaze confidently, and seemed every bit like an old friend.

His living room contained two long, brown sofas; matching ones, arranged around a glass coffee table. The house was wallpapered in an orange and lime pattern, which would have been popular a decade ago in the '60s. Timur's wife,

Divya, languished beside him on the couch.

They'd put out a British high tea, which struck me as being too elaborate for my position in the company.

Nearly every surface of the house was covered in cat hair. I sat ramrod-straight on the sofa, and didn't dare let my suit jacket touch the furry cushions behind me.

"I have to meet a client in an hour," I explained. "I can't stay for long."

"That is quite alright," Divya said in a drawl. Her tongue sounded too large for her mouth. An unfortunate speech impediment, perhaps. "We would not want to keep you from your meeting."

I nodded my thanks.

Timur sat bolt upright like me, but I doubt it was because he was afraid of the cat hair. Divya shifted on the couch, and several great tufts of fur were sent paragliding across the room, before alighting on a mini cupcake that waited at the crown of the high-tea's tiered stand.

The tea was tepid by the time Divya had poured it with trembling wrists. Judging by her stiff body language, it suddenly became apparent that Divya mustn't interact with many people aside from her husband.

The bright midday sunlight streamed in through the living room's open windows. A fly buzzed through the air, but neither of my hosts seemed bothered by it. In the corner of the living room, a litter of cats was reclining. A big grey one was observing me carefully. A pram sat behind them, and I could just spy a kitten sleeping inside it peacefully. It was wrapped tightly in a cloth nappy.

"Have you had the place long?" I asked, realising that I may have befriended Timur too quickly. The middle-aged man watched me closely, with unflinching eye-contact that made me deeply uncomfortable. He picked up the mini cupcake that was covered in hair, and ate it in a single bite.

"We recently acquired it from the previous occupants," he said.

Perhaps it was Timur's ability to speak that had attracted me to him at the work luncheon. We both appreciated the gift of human language. He gestured to Divya, without looking at her.

"Divya recently fell pregnant again, and I wanted to make sure that we had much better furnishings to raise a child."

I sipped at my tea and tried to surreptitiously remove a strand of coarse hair that had lodged itself between my front teeth.

"You're a father?" I said, surprised. "I didn't realise, congratulations."

"Yes, I've been a father many times before," he said with an earnest grin, leaning forward so that his elbows rested on his knees. "It's just that there's been a considerable gap since the last one. We had complications with the last pregnancy."

Divya kicked her feet up in the air, watching her toes as they wriggled. Her hem of her yellow summer dress fell to her mid-thigh, and I had to quickly avert my gaze.

"Many complications," she said. "The ve–"

Timur coughed loudly. The hairs on his thin moustache bristled as he wrinkled his nose from side to side. "I doubt my good colleague wishes to hear about the struggles of having a family."

He held up the teapot and poured for me, without missing

a beat.

A loud cry sounded from down the hall, and Divya groaned. The sleeping kitten sat up, listening to the sound. Divya lay supine for a short moment, and then leapt a great distance from the sofa without propping herself up.

"Were you a gymnast, Divya?" I asked, secretly glad that there was something to distract me from Timur's piercing gaze. She looked at me quizzically, and then wandered down the hallway to the source of the crying.

"Divya doesn't get out much," Timur explained. A look of irritation flashed across his face, but then it was gone. "She has the child to keep her company at least."

"It must be difficult to care for someone who doesn't talk back yet," I replied.

Divya returned, with a baby in her arms. She sat lightly on the sofa.

"It is frustrating that babies cannot walk when they are born," she said. "They are so dependent on you, for so long."

"I suppose you must want to have some time to yourself," I replied.

"Humans are quite strange, do you agree?" she wondered aloud. "When cats are born, they are already prepared to move, and can find the milk or protection of their mother."

"I guess humans are unique."

"Indeed," Timur interjected. "Humans are very special indeed."

In the lull of conversation that followed, I sipped at the new tea Timur had poured for me. His gaze was transfixed on me, and I realised suddenly that he was copying my posture carefully, almost religiously.

Is that what attracted me to him at the party? Was he copying me there as well?

I tried to recall what he had looked like when I saw him across the room. Timur had been holding his disposable cup around the rim, with one hand supporting it underneath. I also did that when I was nervous.

I made a little swirling motion with my right hand. Timur did the same. Perhaps this is why he seemed so disarming, despite his many quirks. I made a mental note to try it with my client later this evening.

The baby was making gasping noises, and I saw that it's face was covered with tufts of cat hair as well.

"He is just hungry," said Divya. She hooked a thumb under her sleeve, and pulled a blue-veined breast out from her summer dress. I felt a cold panic, and quickly averted my gaze back to Timur, who was mimicking my wide-eyed expression. He still wore a smile, however.

"Timur, perhaps you should invest in the new Lint Pic-Up I've been reading about." I suggested. "Some children are allergic to cats, even at a young age."

"That is the other thing that's unusual about humans," said Divya. In my periphery, I could see she wasn't trying to cover herself at all.

"It's strange that we aren't covered in fur?"

"No, it is strange that you are uncomfortable when babies eat."

Timur uncrossed his legs, and I realised that I had done the same thing a few seconds earlier. He tilted his head to the side.

"Does a mother feeding a child make you uncomfortable?" he asked. "That's fascinating. Do other people feel the same way as you do? Is it considered—" he searched for the word on my face, "—taboo?"

"Yes, of course—" I stammered.

I looked at my watch, and saw that half an hour had passed since I arrived. I drank half of my tea, ignoring the wiry hairs that slipped down my throat, and placed the half-full cup and saucer back on the coffee table.

"It's been such a pleasure to join you both. You have a lovely home," I said. Out of the corner of my eye, I saw the big grey cat sit up.

"Look at that," said Timur. He turned and addressed the grey cat in the corner. "Remember that, Mr Whiskers. People seem very uncomfortable around babies feeding." He turned back to me. "Now, is it the baby itself that makes you nervous, or the mother?"

"It's neither really," I said, and collected my satchel from the floor.

"Oh, you're leaving so soon?" Timur asked. He stood as well.

"Yes, well I'm afraid my next client doesn't like to be kept waiting." I made a move to go towards the door, but Divya stood, baby still suckling, and put herself between me and the exit.

"You are afraid?" she asked.

"No," I skirted past, careful not to touch her. "It's just an expression. I'm being polite."

"Please," said Timur. "You must stay and teach us about how to be more polite. I could pour some more of that tea you seemed to be enjoying, yes?"

The offer of more hospitality almost forced me to stay, but

I brushed my guilt aside.

"No, thank you all the same," I bowed slightly, and made it to the front door. I tried the door handle, and realised that Timur had locked the door when we arrived.

The hot summer air blew on my face, tantalisingly close.

I felt a hand on my shoulder, and Timur was at the door beside me.

"Let me get that for you," he said. He made a big show of reaching into his jacket, and then produced a ring of keys. He pushed one of them into the door. It didn't budge.

"Must be the wrong key," he said.

His hot breath washed across my cheek. He tried another key, and shook his head with a laugh.

"You think I'd be able to find it by now."

A third key, and then the latch clicked.

"There you go," Timur said.

"Thank you again for your hospitality," I said.

"No, no." Timur's hand shot into my own hand for a handshake. It felt like a python biting a rat. "Really, the pleasure was all mine. I've learned so much."

I opened the door and stepped outside. The air was clean, and I breathed it in gratefully. The door wheezed shut behind me, and I turned to see Timur standing behind the security screen, watching me. He had his arm firmly around Divya, who was still nursing her baby. They looked for all the world like a normal suburban family. Except for their smiles. Timur's smile was too exaggerated. Divya smiled more normally, but her head wasn't tilted correctly.

I walked briskly up the driveway and to my car parked on the street.

"See you on Monday," Timur called. "If we don't see you before then!"

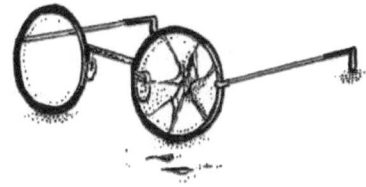

Second Father

Kieran sat facing his old iron bed. Its springs were rusted, and they creaked with every slight movement he made at night. The creature that held the boy's fascination watched him from the shadows underneath the bed.

A handful of sticky sweets sat in Kieran's outstretched hand, his sweat painting the artificial colours across his fingers. The creature made a scratching noise, edging closer and then pausing to watch.

"Good pet."

The creature that crawled from beneath its quilted lair was a mottled purple and bright orange. Hard yellow lumps protruded through the soft skin all over its back. A repulsive smell of spoiled milk lingered about the thing, evidence of its bootleg breakfast that morning. Soiled newspaper clung to the underside of its belly, dripping brown water as it slid forward on two rows of tiny stub legs.

It had no perceivable jaw or mouth, so Kieran was still unsure about how it ingested its food. The creature watched the sweets for a long moment, before burying its face in Kieran's sweaty palm. Kieran felt a gooey sensation, and when the thing moved its head away, his hand was clean and dry.

"Clever boy."

Kieran turned and began writing down notes about his secret pet. Yesterday, he had discovered the thing under an outcrop of rocks, near the shoreline of the Sacred Lake. Kieran had spent hours observing it on his stomach, lying in a puddle. Curiously enough, the creature had nestled in his discarded cap. Enraptured, Kieran had carried it back to his house that rested on the Sacred Lake's shore.

"You aren't a slug with those legs." He whispered to himself, ignoring a thumping sound downstairs. "You can't possibly be Pseudocolochirus, because you have eyes."

There was a cough, and Kieran dropped his pencil. It rolled with a hollow rattle in an arc across the cold floorboards and neatly arrayed notes of paper, towards the door. The muddy boots of Kieran's father prevented the pencil's escape.

Mr Byrne stood hunched over, a silhouette in the doorway. The man lurched forward into the small bedroom. Kieran winced as hours of notes and sketches were kicked out of their perfect rows by his father's boots.

An empty wine glass dangled from two of Mr Byrne's fingers like a cigarette. His small, round spectacles perched delicately on the edge of his nose. The glass reflected the candlelight so brilliantly that his eyes were hidden behind the stark white lenses. Kieran glanced at his pet, still obscured in the shadows. Mr Byrne spoke through the corner of his drooping mouth, the unfortunate symptom of a nervous stroke he'd had five months earlier.

"Supper is ready."

Kieran nodded. A stain on his father's shoe looked almost like a little fish.

"Look at me boy. Head up."

"Can we play after supper?"

Mr Byrne bent down to retrieve a shred of paper out from under his boot, he examined the meticulous sketches.

"This stuff isn't cheap. It's not for documenting your day-dreams."

"Sorry sir."

"Yeah," Mr Byrne jerked his head towards the door, "git."

Kieran scampered past.

* * *

Their meal began with a quiet prayer, but the conversation consisted of the clink of spoons on bowls. Kieran looked at his mother's apron, which still hung on the pantry door: undisturbed for five months. She had been a painter by trade, and the neighbouring farmers had always jostled to purchase her masterpieces whenever they could afford to.

Kieran's mother, however, had died in a terrible accident involving a clumsy stumble, a surprisingly robust paintbrush, and a tragically brittle skull. The entire town mourned the loss of such a vibrant personality, but agreed unanimously that the accidental, crimson painting of the town square was her best abstract piece yet.

Mealtimes had always been loud and joyful when Mrs Byrne was alive, and a menagerie of wildlife had inhabited the garden. Now Mr Byrne's altered plants and biological experiments engulfed the house instead. Kieran had once seen a wallaby grazing in the garden; it had dipped its head down to chew the grass near a particularly nasty breed of Golden Wattle. The wallaby had pulled back, minus its head.

Kieran was twitchy, thinking about his new pet. He was hoping he might smuggle it outside, and amuse himself with a game he used to play with his mother.

A familiar scraping noise resonated from the kitchen doorway. Both Kieran and Mr Byrne glanced across slowly and saw the thing, outlined in the doorway.

The dusty grandfather clock in the corner paused, pendulum in mid-arc. Mr Byrne sat with his spoon halfway to his mouth, jaw slack. His watery pupils comically resembled the eyes of the creature in front of him. Then the spell was suddenly broken.

Mr Byrne stood up too quickly, and his chair reared backwards on two legs before crashing into the bench behind him. Dashing around the table to snatch the thing, he trod on a piece of neglected lettuce from their dinner and fell.

Kieran sipped his soup carefully.

Mr Byrne stood again, ignoring the odd angle his foot was at, and scooped up the creature, holding it aloft like an idol. Kieran stopped eating.

"He's my friend."

"This..." Mr Byrne's spectacles had become foggy with condensation as he admired the discovery. "I'm going to be someone."

"Is he special?" The boy asked, but Mr Byrne didn't hear. He was already limping away with surprising speed: cradling the creature like a child in an egg-and-spoon race.

These days, Kieran's father spent most of his free time locked up in the wine cellar he had converted into a laboratory. Kieran crept after his father down the cramped, stagnant staircase. Kieran recoiled from the mould that covered the walls. One strain of black stachybotrys mold seemed like it was trying to communicate.

Normally, a large wooden door with five keyholes disqualified entry into Mr Byrne's cramped laboratory, but tonight the door was open. Mr Byrne placed the thing in a surgical tray to prevent its escape. Rows of steel tools lined the walls, arranged in order of size: from two-man timber saws, down to tiny display pins. Mr Byrne hummed along to himself as he jauntily picked a selection of instruments with crude tips and barbs.

"Will you hurt him?" Kieran asked.

"I wish you would refrain from referring to it as a *him*," Mr Byrne replied, putting his tools down and lifting the creature up to gaze underneath. "The specimen appears to be asexual." He pressed two fingers into the pet's tender, swollen sides.

It whimpered.

"You can see it appears to be carrying offspring."

Mr Byrne lifted Kieran's pet up to his lips, and planted a wet kiss on what could have been its face. As he pulled away a string of mucus trailed between his slanting lips and the creature.

"I'm going to be famous, m'boy." Slime dripped from Mr Byrne's mouth as he spoke. He wiped the substance away with his sleeve.

"Tomorrow, I intend to catch the morning locomotive, and present my findings to the National Organisation of Biological Sciences." He was talking in a rush, his eyes glancing about, unseeing. "You'll have to stay with Mrs de Barra after school."

"Will you play with him?" Kieran asked, as he watched his pet tremble on the cold metal tray.

"Those ponces at the organisation don't recognise any discovery until it's cut up, sterilised, and diagrammed."

Mr Byrne took a long, hooked instrument and tapped Kieran's nose to illustrate his point. At that, the creature made a gurgling noise and attacked Mr Byrne.

Kieran was looking at his nose, so he never saw his pet compress into itself, and was not privy to its remarkable jump. The thing landed on Mr Byrne's face, and then it crawled down his throat.

Mr Byrne's slanting jaw hung agape. His eyebrows perched up high behind his opaque spectacles. A definite lump travelled down his oesophagus. Tiny rows of legs could be seen bulging out either side of his neck, as they attempted to swim against his gag reflex. Mr Byrne collapsed on the ground gurgling, and then fell silent.

* * *

It was a sunny day, and the purple flowers that speckled the hills were especially bright. Ladies in long, dark dresses floated to the ceremony with their partners, concentrating on the slow steps they took. The music of flutes and stringed instruments drifted past the crowd.

The priest began his address, and Mr Byrne was lowered into his grave in a simple, open casket. Kieran peered down at his father's stiff body as it descended, hands laced together over his stomach.

Kieran saw a finger twitch.

Then, Mr Byrne's hands began to unfold.

Mrs de Barra, standing nearby, had noticed it too, and fainted with a flourish. Unfortunately, she fell forwards into the open grave. The crowd rushed forward to peek into the pit while the priest prayed on, oblivious.

Mr Byrne's stomach was convulsing like an earthquake. Emerging from the mouth of the corpse were half-a-dozen creatures, similar to Kieran's pet.

Kieran pulled a notepad out of his back pocket and began to take notes. These creatures were different to the original. They were a shade of dark blue, and now jumped proficiently.

The boy marvelled as one of them leapt out of the grave, and landed next to his foot. He picked it up, and held it aloft like his father once had. This new creature stared back at him.

Its eyes were white, circular, and shiny, almost like spectacles. A small, slanting mouth was now visible. Kieran placed it inside his inner coat pocket.

Perhaps his new father might play with him.

Feathers

I leaked out from the earth at the stroke of dawn. The small parish bells rang a sombre scale in the cold, crisp air. The final note echoed out into an overcast sky. A smell of dirt and peat clung to me as I leaned against a stunted tree that grew in the corner of the churchyard.

The chapel was built precariously on an untillable hillside, and a procession of people now meandered down and away from the church, towards the countryside township below. The stench of fertiliser hung thickly in the air.

I watched the sun climb high into the sky.

The distant fire appeared atop the dark mountains in the distance: mountains I didn't know the name of. With nothing better to do, I pulled myself up onto the strongest branch of the twisted tree, and sat there through the entire day, and then the night.

I haven't done this since I was a child, I realised.

The night was dark. A stray cat walked past my quiet spot, and I called out to it. The cat's tail rose up sharp and straight, and it hissed in my direction, before dashing out of sight, down the hillside, and between the scrub that littered the dirt road down there.

I watched the sun rise and set several more times.

Each morning, the parish priest would make the journey up the hill on knobbly knees, assisted by a young boy who stood resolutely under his armpit.

The sun rose and set, and then the churchyard was visited again. Two scrawny youths with shovels dug a hole in the earth between the rows of toothy tombstones. When the sun's light had risen sufficiently to touch the small township below, I saw the grey smudges of people in the distance begin moving about.

A procession up the hillside began, with four burly farmers carrying a small casket on their shoulders. I leapt down from my observation spot, and sat near the hole the boys were finishing. The casket was placed in the yard, and the priest with the weak knees said a few words.

The ceremony was too short. The priest seemed weary. He slurred his words in a hurry to complete them. The farmers began lowering the casket into the ground in the middle of his address. A young woman blew steam into her hands, while an old man hopped from foot to foot in the cold air. Frost from the night still clung to blades of grass. A small girl wept openly.

The crowd dispersed, and began the weary descent down the hillside once more. A bag of grain was handed over as payment to both of the youths with shovels, and to the priest. The grave was filled in, and patted down. A simple wooden cross was hammered into the earth, sans name. There were other crosses strewn throughout the property. They equalled the number of stone tombstones.

I remained in my tree, and watched the town below. It was harvest time, but there weren't enough workers. The yellow fields of wheat should have been harvested by now, but the town was still surrounded by large swathes of crop that would soon rot. From afar, I watched the farmers as they began to trickle inside once the sun was beginning to set. The bells rang the evening toll, which is when I saw the spirit of a woman spill out of the fresh ground where she had been buried that morning. I held out my hand to help, but she battered it away.

"Are you alright?" I asked.

She sat, her body glowing faintly as she mimicked the action of panting, but she had no lungs to fill with air.

"You look familiar," she said at last.

Her nose was freckled, and her left eye hung lazily in its socket. She had auburn hair, and narrow hips. Her clothing was a shadow that moved across her body, a suggestion, but nothing that could definitely be called a dress.

"I think I had a dream about you," I replied, examining her grey eyes.

She stood up and brushed the shadows that clung to her, but there was no dirt that needed to be loosened.

"Huh," she said.

I showed her my tree, and she smiled politely as I

demonstrated how to climb up to the best limb to sit on.

"Have you been here long?" she asked.

"Perhaps a week? Perhaps a month?"

"You aren't certain?"

"I haven't found the desire to do much other than sit here," I replied. "Do you understand what happened to you? Do you remember anything?"

"I think I died," she said. "I can't remember much else."

"Me neither," I said. "I figured it would come back to me."

"Are you going to stay up there?" she asked.

"I suppose so," I replied.

She turned back towards the township, and watched it until the last of the farmers trudged home from the fields.

"I think I might go down to that small town, and see if I can figure out who I am."

Her long hair flicked in the wind, and I felt a deep pang of guilt.

"I'll come with," I offered, and jumped down from the stunted tree. We made our way down the dirt path, towards the town. It was a short walk, but steep. I was surprised the priest didn't need to be carried up the hill in a cart. I kicked a small stone as we walked down towards the town, and tripped over it neatly when it wouldn't budge.

The lady saw me stagger, and laughed pleasantly as I jumped back to my feet.

"Huh," I said. We continued down the hill. I stopped at a small bush and tried to pull a leaf free. It swayed gently under my touch, as though the wind was stirring it, but it wouldn't pull free.

"Let me try," the lady said. She held her hand next to the

leaf, and waited. The evening wind was beginning to stir, and the leaf billowed this way and that, passing through her hand. She tried to grab at it, but couldn't.

"I'm cold," she said. She stood up, and swaddled her shoulders in a shadow.

Instinctively, I reached out to put my arm around her, but caught myself when she flinched.

"My apologies."

The town was in a sorry state as we walked along the main thoroughfare. Someone chopped wood out the front of their house, and laid it in neat rows beneath a thatched shed roof. The mill had been halted for the day. Two old women, perhaps forty-five, were gossiping with the miller, while pretending to negotiate a price for their grain.

"I hear lavender cures it," said the woman with a more pronounced stoop.

"Good luck finding any at this time of year," the miller replied.

"We've been saving it up," she replied. "Just in case anyone else starts getting sick."

"I think I might offer some to the Fletchers' little girl," the other lady said. "She might have breathed the same air as her parents."

"Poor thing," the miller said. He nodded out over their heads at the small girl who had been crying at the funeral.

"Poor thing," the spectral woman next to me echoed.

She went over to the child, who was sitting in the dirt, cuddling a small doll made of straw that had been bundled to look like limbs and a head. The spectre placed her hand on the child's head, and stroked it delicately.

"Were you a mother?" I asked her.

"I must have been," she replied. "Do I look old enough to be one?"

I couldn't possibly fathom her age, I realised. There was a smoothness, a glossiness to her features. It was like judging the age of a passing cloud.

"I think you were a fine mother," I replied.

The smell of bread wafted across the wind, and so the child with stained cheeks stood and trudged towards a nearby house.

"You must have lived somewhere nearby," I said, but the lady was lost in thought, staring after the child. A bitter wind blew a nearby shutter open and closed. Its loud, wooden knock brought her out of the trance.

"Let's get out of the chill," she suggested.

The miller was feeding his old, mustard-coloured horse with the husks left-over from the day. He patted its thin neck, and then locked the door of the mill. As he trudged away, we followed him wordlessly.

The town had three crooked main streets that intersected near a crank pump at its centre. Many of the houses were now derelict, with planks of wood barring the windows and doors.

An enormous inn stood opposite the pump. The miller washed his face and hands at the pump, walked up the sloping road, and then pushed the inn's door open. The warm light of a fire leapt out across the ground. Laughter and singing filled the air for a moment, and was quickly extinguished when the miller closed the door behind him.

We climbed the few steps to the wooden door, and tried the door tentatively. The rope handle felt as heavy as lead, and refused to budge. I gave the door a firm push, but it didn't move.

"Blessed Mother!" the lady yelled in frustration. She kicked the door, but her foot bounced off it without a sound.

"Perhaps there's another way in?" I suggested.

She blew a strand of hair from her face, and nodded. We turned from the doorway, which was when it opened. A thin, hairy patron was tossed outside by the immense innkeeper. The unfortunate patron narrowly caught himself before falling on his face. His head whipped around.

"Why'd you do that?" he complained, nearly cross-eyed from the alcohol.

The spectral lady slipped under the burly innkeeper's arm, which was wedged against the doorframe, and made it inside. I ducked after her, but found myself caught between the doorframe and his body odour.

"Help!"

The lady turned, and reached out a hand to pull me through.

"Henry, I've got mouths to feed," said the innkeeper. "You owe me at least ten shillings."

I was desperately trying to scramble through the space between the innkeeper's knee and forearm, but my hips were stuck.

"I'm good for it!" the man outside said, pulling himself nearly upright. "The fletching business is going to pick up now..." He trailed off when he saw the innkeeper's face.

"Those were good folk," the innkeeper said. "Simon, rest his soul, worked himself to death to feed his family. He didn't need a pathetic brother to leeching off him."

"That's not true! I fed myself." The drunkard tried to force his way back into the inn, but the innkeeper was wedged securely against it.

I twisted through the narrowing gap as the innkeeper began to close the door. I kicked my legs out, while the lady tugged at my bicep.

"You didn't have to do seasonal labour around here," the innkeeper hissed through the door. "You could've gone a few towns over and found real work, but you were happy doing odd jobs and living off your brother's generosity, may he rest in peace. I dearly hope you pick yourself up and do him proud. Until then, you're banned from this inn."

My foot caught against Henry's torso as he argued with the innkeeper. I kicked off him, and sailed through the doorway just as the innkeeper door slammed shut in the drunkard's face.

With the door closed and barred, the innkeeper returned to the sea of men and women who sat on stools at small tables. As I lay on the floor of the inn, catching my breath, I could finally take in our surroundings. The beer frothed from tankards, and a large roast pig sat on the large counter, being served by a thickset woman. The knocks and protests of the drunkard outside went ignored for a long time.

The lady and I found a quiet corner of the inn. I chewed on my thumbnail while the lady looked around at the faces.

"Were these people at my burial?" she asked.

"I recognise some of them," I said. The two young men who had dug her grave were singing a bawdy, out-of-tune ditty.

"They look happy," she said. "Shouldn't they look sad?"

"I don't know." I remembered the wooden crosses littering the churchyard. "Perhaps there's been a lot of death here recently, and they're trying to forget about it?"

We watched the drinking and carousing for a time. As the sky began to darken, the tables and chairs were quickly pushed to the sides of the room, nearly crushing us as we scrambled to evade them. An old man pulled out a fiddle, and everyone present began to pair off and dance.

"To the Fletchers!" someone yelled, holding a tankard aloft. The cry was echoed throughout the inn, and then the dancing began. Tables were bumped and drinks were spilled on the wooden floor as the dancers twirled and spun in the cramped confines of the alehouse.

"Would you like to dance?" I offered, and held out a glowing hand.

She looked at me for a bar, and then took it.

We stayed clear of the windmill of bodies that spun in the middle of the dancefloor, swaying in the corner instead. The shadows across our bodies flowed with our movements. She twirled for me, and then our hands met again.

A young couple danced nearby. In the candlelight, the almost-man held his partner awkwardly. His eyes constantly glanced between his feet, and the hand that held her waist.

"Why do people fall in love?" my dance partner asked.

I chewed on it. "To be happy, I suppose."

One of the men swung his partner into another pair. She quickly apologised, and then berated him loudly as she exited the dance floor.

"Marriage isn't always happy though."

"Perhaps people don't realise that, going into it."

"Maybe."

Her feet had slowed, and we separated, watching the other

dancers instead.

"Is the purpose of marriage to have children?" she wondered aloud. "I can't stop thinking about that poor child we saw earlier."

"I'm sure that's part of it," I said. "I'd love to have children one day."

"Can you?" she asked suddenly, looking me up and down. "I mean, the way that you are?"

I touched the shadows across my own body, looking for a part or opening. It was like trying to divide water in a bucket. I dug, but didn't feel anything substantial that I could lift to examine myself beneath those shadows.

"So, no children then," she said, once my digging had gone on long enough.

"I suppose not," I admitted. "Why does it matter though?"

"Because," she said. "I'm wondering if we should stay married or not."

The dancers swept through the hall, and the women were dipped as the song concluded. There was a round of drinks ordered, and a toast to the Fletchers again.

"We're married?" I asked.

"Or were," she replied.

"How long have you known?"

"Since you tried to hold me as we walked down here," she admitted. "Or maybe since I saw that little girl. I knew it for certain once everyone started referring to the dead Fletchers."

"Why are you certain that we're the Fletchers?" I asked.

"Because I can see feathers stuck in your hair," she replied. "Or at least, whatever it is I'm seeing that looks like hair."

I reached up and touched my crown. There were small

watery shadows up there, similar to my clothing. A hint of something from my past, and nothing more. I felt behind me, and sat down on a discarded table at the edge of the room.

I gazed deeply into her lazy eye. I remembered what she smelled like while we sat plucking chickens out the front of our small cottage. I remembered her name. Agnes.

"Is this fate? Or destiny?" I asked. "How did we end up here, together? I could have walked away from that church, followed the path down through the town, and gone towards the dark mountains without ever seeing you again."

"Maybe it's a cruel joke," Agnes said bitterly. She wiped her eyes, but there weren't any tears. "I figured we'd be clothed in white, and whisked away someplace nice."

"Maybe there's something else we need to do first," I suggested, placing a hand on Agnes' shoulder. It felt cool, like the morning air.

"I just don't know." Agnes brushed the hand away gently. "I promised to be with you until death, and now here it is, and here we are, and I have no idea what we're supposed to do now."

A deep realisation washed across me in that moment. There was no work that needed to be done. We had worked ourselves to poor health for our daughter, but now we couldn't provide for her any longer. There are no coins in the afterlife.

I looked back at the dancers as they swayed and held each other. The young man was gaining confidence with his partner. He had begun to laugh, and could bring his gaze up to her eyes briefly, before quickly dropping them to his feet again.

"I think the soul needs others," I said at last. "The thought of being alone while I figure out this new life...well, that seems more frightening to me."

Her arms shot out, and suddenly she had buried her nose into the shadows of my chest. It was like being enveloped by a light breeze.

"Thank goodness," she said. "I thought we didn't have any reason to remain together."

We stood there, as the inn's patrons began to leave. Some were crying. Others talked, gossiped, and yelled good night to each other as they staggered home.

"I want to stay here for now, for Isabella's sake," she said. "Then we can decide."

I nodded. "For Isabella."

We watched our daughter grow for nine years in the care of my useless brother, Henry. She grew into a young woman before our eyes: sitting in the front yard, plucking feathers, and whittling wood six days a week to pay for her bread, and my brother's drinking. Her cough began shortly after her fifteenth birthday, and it stopped a month before her sixteenth. Her casket was decorated with lavender as the townspeople carried it solemnly up the little hill.

She was buried with a wooden cross, in a plot of soil next to the priest with knobby knees. We wept alongside the young man who had fancied her, but hadn't saved up enough to propose. Then, when the bells struck morning the next day, we welcomed our daughter with a ghostly embrace, and quiet words of explanation.

For a long time, we sat as a family in the branches of the twisted tree that overlooked the town. Until one morning, when we walked through the sleeping town for the last time, and began our trek towards the dark mountains that have no name.

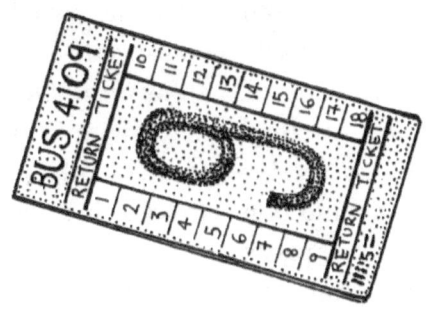

Last Stop

I've sold insurance all my life. That's what I tell people who ask about my profession. In reality, however, it's felt like many lifetimes. Working in sales has the ability to suck anyone dry. My father, rest him, had been adamant that I should go into real estate like he had.

"Get into property, buy up the old palm oil land, and you'll be ready to build a city of investment houses once the economy flatlines again," he'd told me. "You have to live it and breathe it though. You have to know the game, so you know when to bite. You have to starve yourself of everything else, so you can gorge yourself when the time is right."

He'd told me variations of that every day, up until I'd

earned my undergraduate certificate in sales. He died the day afterwards.

"It was the shame that killed him, not the heart disease," the doctor told my mother. "Shame is taking a whole generation of parents. It's the new cancer."

I'm inclined to disagree. I think *insurance salesmanship* should be the next disease registered with WHO. It's gotten into my marrow, you see. I went for a blood test last week, and the phlebotomist could only extract a fine red powder from me, suspended in clear plasma.

My boss, Mr Timur, is a particular man with particular needs. I bring him warm milk each morning before he'll let me begin my calls. He watches us through perspex, munching on dry biscuits shaped like fish.

A group of disgruntled employees, working their seventh Christmas in a row, once tried to defenestrate him. He'd been picked up and tossed through the upper open window where he liked to recline. Then he plummeted gracefully, feet first. Dropping as naturally as the palm branches do, which line our office's view of the city cemetery.

My boss had then taken the elevator back up to the fifth floor, and the employees had gone back to their desks.

There is no escape, I'd realised. The pay was too good, and our boss was immortal.

Each afternoon, I've waited outside the office for the bus with my fellow commuters. Many of them are old. Dad would have been handing out property brochures while he waited. But I'm not my father, so instead I closed my eyes, and enjoyed the sounds of traffic. The revving of engines is a symphony compared to the noise of phones constantly ringing, and customers shouting.

I know I probably sound obsessed, mentioning my father so much. Truthfully, I'm very content. I don't have the energy to be angry, or sad, or hopeful. In fact, there is only one I want in my life: to sell our company's *Platinum* life insurance package. It has a list of benefits that are 34-pages long, but I've never met a soul who could afford it.

Mr Timur managed to sell the package, and it more-or-less pushed him to the position of CEO. It is a laurel every salesperson at the company strives to achieve. The company-paid commission for selling it would be enough to buy any home in the city. And so, every day, while I wait for my bus, I imagine what it would feel like to sell the Platinum package.

My evening bus has been the same for the past year. It's the only black city bus I've ever seen. Most of the buses in our city's fleet have been modernised to a cool cyan exterior, with a faint air conditioning system.

My bus arrived on the dot. The punctuality of the bus alone makes me proud to ride it, despite its ancient exterior. My bus driver is always the same: a stoic old man, which I have no complaints about. Every evening, he sizes me up with a hard stare when I board his bus, and then he shakes his head.

"Not dead yet?" he always asks.

The joke never ceases to amuse me, and I laugh all the way to my seat. The fact that he asks, shows me that he understands my plight as a salesman. The fact that he's willing to say it every day, tells me that we've built a lasting rapport. I suppose I'd even consider him to be one of my closest friends.

Along the ceiling of the bus are small windows, which remain open to prevent everyone from frying. No problem.

The bus is powered by a small diesel engine that is concealed somewhere in the rear, and the fumes it produces nearly caused me to pass out the first time I rode it. I can live with it: the leaded petrol helps me to appreciate how clean the air usually is, by comparison. My favourite seat is situated above one of the wheel housings, and so it tends to scald any bare skin. This doesn't trouble me, because it means my favourite seat is always available. In fact, I have only one complaint about my evening commute.

I don't like the temple road.

We pass it every day, and despite the long hours I work, I have never once felt tempted to sleep on the stretch of the journey that takes us past the temple road.

Today is no different.

It appears for a few heartbeats, as the bus naturally decelerates up an incline. There is a faint dirt road that winds away from the asphalt: cut into the dense jungle, and just wide-enough to accommodate the bus. The dirt road climbs up and out of sight, towards the site of the old temple that used to watch over our valley.

Despite my best efforts to look away, my eyes always linger on that dirt road as we pass.

Two cheap faux-limestone statues guard this path, like the lions before a Chinatown. Both statues have been worn down beyond repair, and warrant replacement. The right-hand one is a stump. It's a nub of feet, a torso, and nothing else: cracked in half by the frequent rain and unforgiving sun. The one on the left has fared better. Half of its body remains, cracked from the forehead, down to the shoulder, leaving most of the detailing intact. Perhaps they had once been gargoyles. It's hard to say. The only feature I can ascertain for certain is a single eye, opened wide, as though the statue was surprised.

I will always stare into that eye.

Then, when I break my eyes away, bleary from a long day at work, there is a moment, however brief, where my driver checks me in the mirror, and I realise that every passenger has turned to look at me. Then, the driver will carry on past the secret road, and once our wheels touch the asphalt again, I will finally allow myself to fall into the fitful slumber of a vigilant commuter.

This particular afternoon, however, I felt the weight of sleep entangle me like a net, dragging me down towards unconsciousness. Perhaps I had been thinking about my father too much recently, and those emotions from my youth were plaguing me once more. Perhaps it was the blood test last week, sapping what little strength remained.

Regardless of the reason, I stupidly allowed myself to relax. Just as we approached those ruined statues, and I felt the gaze of every passenger flick in my direction, my chin dropped to my chest for the briefest of moments.

I was awoken a moment later as the bus hit the temple road. The driver had swung the wheel hard, and a cheer went up from all the passengers except me. Our bus tipped up onto two wheels to take the turn at the last second. The bus driver pulled down the radio broadcaster that was wired into the dashboard of the bus, and spoke as clearly as he could through the ancient machinery.

"As you can see today folks, we're finally joined by our tag-along, and can skip ahead to the main attraction this evening."

"Hurray!" sang an infant in its mother's arms.

We drove quickly up the temple road. The jungle hemmed us in on both sides: two giant walls of green foliage that lashed past the open windows as we sped along in a reckless, uphill spiral. The driver turned each corner with ease. Each bend arrived so suddenly, I was certain he was steering on instinct and memory alone. Just as quickly as the dirt-road journey had begun, it finished. The driver applied the brakes gently, and we pulled up in front of the old temple. The driver turned around with an uncharacteristic smile.

"Last stop."

I disembarked with the passengers, as did the bus driver. He nodded a greeting to me, and I nodded back. He had been waiting for me. I held my briefcase to my chest for comfort.

The old temple had been on the restoration waiting list for a decade, and its foundations had collapsed in the meantime. It now leaned heavily against the craggy hillside behind it, and much of the delicate stone roof had collapsed inward.

The other passengers walked on ahead, and the bus driver waved for me to follow him. I saw that the sun was now low over the horizon, and the bus driver and I cast long shadows ahead of us. The other passengers didn't cast shadows at all.

Was this the bus exchange point? Would we wait under the howls of the forest monkeys for the next driver to arrive, and take over the route?

I realised something was wrong when the mother and daughter ahead of me climbed atop a shattered temple pillar, and began to walk along it. They climbed into a second storey window. Two young boys climbed through what had once been perfectly square windows, and chased each other through the inclined temple's interior.

The bus driver climbed through the same window, and I hesitated.

"I think there's been some sort of mistake." I said. The comforting black bus was far behind us, and I desperately wanted to return to it.

"There's no mistake," the driver replied. His old brown eyes crinkled into a half smile. "I've been wanting to bring you here for a long, long time."

I couldn't remember the last time someone had spoken with such warmth to me, so I crawled through after him.

"Is this some sort of initiation? Is it a rewards system with local transport?"

"It's a ceremony," he replied.

"Are you a privatised wing of transport? No, that can't be right. I hadn't heard about any sort of initiation before. Are you partners with Garuda Airlines? I hear their facilities are excellent."

My driver let out a long sigh, and kept climbing the temple interior.

As we ascended, I saw how much damage the temple had sustained. The interior had once been filled with scores of short pillars, holding the roof aloft in a fascinating display of ancient architecture. Many had now crumbled, and a cold wind blew through the lower levels of the temple.

We continued upwards, and into an uneven chamber that smelled damp. A stalactite dripped from the roof. The other passengers now carried a solemn air as they walked. My driver pulled out a torch to illuminate the darkness ahead, which was when I understood where I was. The temple had tipped into the hillside, and broken into a natural cave. The way forward was a serpentine tunnel, into the depths of the earth.

I followed the driver.

We descended further into the immense chamber beneath the earth. Our path fell away to either side. As we journeyed deeper and deeper, I became aware of a buzzing in my ears, as though I were straining to hear silence.

The natural walkway we followed was strung between tower-like fingers of stone. A harsh karst landscape of silicon ran below us and our path. The earth was a sickly colour here, reflecting upon itself, like a cascade of antique mirrors. The occasional water pool was stagnant and milky. I felt nauseous looking at it.

Something rose up ahead, out of the alien environment.

A chair had been carved into the stone. It was an awful thing, cut from the same stone as the cavern. As I approached, I nearly tripped over hunched shapes that were curled up against the ground: my fellow passengers. The buzzing in my ears grew in its urgency.

The passengers bowed low to the chair, and whispered requests through mouths that required no air. The whispers overlapped, and fifty voices became a buzz in the air. One young man rocked like a metronome against the floor.

At this point, the very fibres of my being screamed that I should leave. This was not something I was supposed to witness, no matter how reassuring my driver was. Yet, I was drawn inexplicably forward by the same force that drew my gaze towards the dirt road every evening. A singular thought was lodged in my mind: *how valuable might this land be, if it was added to an investment portfolio and allowed to mature?*

The buzzing in the air stopped, as something atop the great

stone chair turned to look at me. It glowed a faint blue-green against the red stone of the cavern. It resembled a giant human, but only just. The creature had no nose, and at its chin was a thin and pointed beak. I gripped my briefcase tightly for comfort. The creature on the immense chair spoke.

"A new arrival. Is this the one you mentioned to me, Tantry?"

The bus driver bowed low. "It certainly is, oh great spirit. He has climbed aboard many times before."

The spirit's eyes sat uncomfortably wide on its face. The whites of its eyes had turned black, leaving just the bright green irises. It turned its head to examine me, and then recoiled.

"Tantry, look again at this creature you brought me."

The driver paused. His hand reached out to touch me, and then he recoiled. The other passengers gasped.

"That's right Tantry, you idiot. You brought me a breather."

Tantry's eyes were wide, and he fell down before the great spirit.

"Great spirit, I had no idea. Each day this man has stepped onto my bus, and I knew he wasn't ready. How can he even see the bus? There must be something wrong with the spell you placed on it."

The spirit puffed itself up to look even bigger. Blue-green feathers were beginning to sprout across its form. Long, brown toenails stuck out from where it squatted on the chair. The arms remained somewhat human, but were transitioning to the wings of a great bird.

"Does he still have a pulse?" the great spirit asked.

Tantry pushed two fingers roughly into my jugular. After

three minutes, there was a single heartbeat.

"He's still alive." Tantry staggered backwards, and wiped a few beads of sweat from his brow. "You should be dead. I've looked into the eyes of countless spirits, and you look more dead than any of them. I've ferried hundreds of spirits, and I've never made a mistake before." He turned to the other passengers, his hands begging. "Back me up guys, we all thought he was going to bite the dust any minute. We all saw him die on the bus."

"Idiot!" the great spirit yelled. "I told you it takes time for a spirit to naturally leave its body."

"So, you're all dead?" I asked.

"Of course we're dead, you idiot." The words were hurled by a young lady in billowing black clothes and headscarf, who I had fancied once or twice on the commute home. "How could you not realise we were dead? We're practically translucent."

She wasn't wrong. They all wore shifting clothing, and if I concentrated, I could see through them. I'd just always thought it was eye strain from my computer.

The situation was beginning to dawn on me. I looked at each of my fellow passengers, and came to the sinking realisation that this hillside was going rapidly devalue, if people found out that ghosts lived here.

"Tantry, I'm very disappointed in you," the great spirit said. It waddled forward, off the great stone chair. The other passengers scrambled to get out of its way.

My driver turned and ran, but he was quickly set upon by the spirit. I watched, aghast, as the spirit removed Tantry's arm and swallowed it like an owl guzzling a worm. Tantry screamed, holding the bloody stump where his arm had once been.

In that moment, I felt an urgency deep inside myself that I hadn't felt before. It was an electricity, a singular desire. I leapt forward, and spread my arms wide, putting myself between the spirit and Tantry.

"I'd like to say one final thing to the driver, if you don't mind," I said. "Then you may kill us both."

The other spirits watched in a reverent silence.

"Very well," the great spirit said with the approximation of a smile.

I backed away from the great spirit's towering form, and bent over the moaning body of my bus driver.

"Tantry," I whispered. "Maybe you didn't know this, but your bus route was one of the few things that has kept me going all these years. I now realise you were trying to lure me into a spiritual pyramid scheme, but despite that I'd like to offer you something."

Tantry paused his moaning for a brief moment. The other lesser spirits leaned forward to listen.

"Tantry," I began.

"Yes?"

"This isn't something I usually just give away."

"Tell me."

"I want you to really understand and cherish what I'm offering."

"Hurry up," said the great spirit.

"Tantry." I took a deep breath. "Have you by any chance purchased life insurance? It could really benefit your loved ones in a time of sudden and unexpected death. Usually you need a cooling off period before you can claim, but if you upgrade to the *Platinum* package, and sign this paperwork right now, I can give you a promotional code that will provide maximum benefits to your loved ones."

Tantry coughed up blood. Then, he said the single most beautiful sentence I've ever heard.

"I'll take the *Platinum* package."

I bent down there and then on the cavern floor, and popped the latches of my briefcase. Inside, the paperwork for the *Platinum* package sat in sealed plastic. I tore the packet open. The paper smelled like freshly sanded wood. I removed my best pen from its box, and helped Tantry hold it. I couldn't tell which of us was shaking more.

"We'll just write your name here on the dotted line," I said.

Tantry moved his arm sloppily, and I could see his eyes roll listlessly.

"I'll get you to write the date here." I carried the pen along the page and dated the document. The numbers practically sizzled as we wrote them together, and I realised that this date had become more important to me, than my own birthday.

Tantry dropped the pen as he died, and I dropped Tantry.

"Look at this," I said, my eyes wide with excitement. I felt a fervour in my blood and was finding it difficult to breathe.

Is this what it feels like to win a Nobel prize? Your life culminating in a single moment? I wiped my eyes, and bowed deeply to the great spirit. "Thank you."

"You're welcome," said the great spirit. He pointed a long toenail at my throat like a sword. "When your spirit is awakened, you won't remember much. However, I'm willing to help you resolve any desires you might have. They don't call me the Gift-Giver for nothing."

"Why do they call you that?" I asked.

"Many come here and trade their souls for a wish. I grant whatever is in my power, and in turn these lesser spirits let me feed on their desires. That way I can become more powerful, and grant stronger wishes. We're a community here."

He waddled over to the young lady, and caressed her head with a long, dirty talon. The great spirit deftly pulled a thin strand of silk from the hair. He ran it between two grotesque toenails, and pulled on it gently. I saw the strand go taut and glow for a brief moment. It was embedded in the young lady's chest. The strand was much lighter than air. I saw a tiny pinpoint of light travel from her chest, along the string, and travel back out the way we'd come.

"Anything that keeps a soul rooted to this earth can be traced," the great spirit said. "You only need to know how to look. I grant one wish, and then I am able to devour the single thread of that desire."

"How would they know or care whether the wish was granted?" I asked, "Since you devour the desire itself? It's like a bait-and-switch sales tactic. People will end up thinking that they've their desires filled, but they don't have them anymore."

The great spirit waddled towards me as fast as his toenails would allow. "I've run out of patience, you disgusting breather."

Without ceremony or fanfare, his toenail lanced my throat open, and I died.

I'm not going to lie, though: it felt a lot better than I imagined it would. For example, a generalised anxiety that I'd carried since I was in my early twenties just upped and vanished. As I died, I saw my life as an explosion of light ahead of me, seeping from the gash in my neck.

"Welcome to the afterlife," sang a thousand voices. I heard a choir and stringed instruments.

A montage of images and moments flashed in front of me. For someone who lived a complex and interesting life, I'm sure it would have been a kaleidoscope of memories, a veritable panorama of activity and moments.

For me, it was lots of moments centred around my desk and the bus ride home, as the powers that be desperately tried to stitch together some sort of powerful montage of my life. There was another bright flash.

"Here are your happy memories," the voices sang.

I only saw one thing: Tantry and I signing the paperwork together.

* * *

I sat up and out of my body.

I was in a cave, but I could see through the darkness easily. Above me, a stone throne had been carved into the rockface. A creature sat upon the chair, looking down at me with a fearful expression.

"What is the meaning of this?" it asked.

"Hello," I said, greeting the ugly man-bird.

The strange creature approached me. Its face illuminated in my glow.

"You awoke as a great spirit?" it asked in a disgusted voice. "How? How? Tell me how!" The ugly bird flew in my face, and I swatted it away with a hand. I only meant to discourage it, but the bird flew across the room and hit the cave wall, hard.

"Oops, sorry about that," I said with a chuckle. I looked

back down at my old body. My almond eyes were cold, and frozen open in shock. On my face, however, there was an unmistakable grin.

The bird limped towards me.

"Your desires," it said. "Show them to me."

The bird ran a disgusting toenail along my chest, searching for something.

"Stop that."

"There's nothing," it said in disbelief. "There's nothing left to you. How are you so empty? How did you manage to detach yourself so completely from all humans, all dreams, all desires?"

I didn't know what to say, so I stood and quietly excused myself, leaving the bird. As I exited the cave, I found a group of small spirits that looked familiar, all sitting at the entrance of the cavern. A tiny, frightened spirit who was clothed in the shadows of a bus driver's uniform waved to me.

"Can we follow you?" he asked.

I walked over and patted him on the shoulder, and we ascended up and into the sunlight. We climbed through an old building, and then out to stand on a hillside overlooking a rural city.

"How beautiful," I said.

I looked down at the other spirits, who looked up at me in disbelief.

"You're so fat, and majestic," the little one said. "What should we call you, great spirit?"

"You can call me Ni," I said, and patted my ample gut.

It Figurines

If anyone happened to pass by *Our Lady of Knock High School* last Wednesday, around lunchtime, they would have noticed a crowd of teenagers standing in a perfect circle beneath the shade of the playground's leopard trees. A plague of gnats buzzed through the humid afternoon air, but we resolutely ignored them.

"I'm telling you, it's true," said the new girl, Jamie Smith.

She had flowing blonde hair that she let down whenever the teachers weren't looking. Jamie could've gotten a casual job as a shampoo model, and the boys had noticed. I twirled a strand of my own hair in irritation. Jamie sat at the centre of the circle, applying a new coat of bright pink lip gloss, and addressed us all in a hush.

"At my last school, my ex and I used these a bunch of times to visit each other in our dreams. It was great. It's only twenty bucks to use one of them for the night, and then you bring them back the next day, so I can recharge them."

"How do they work?" I asked. "How's a statue supposed to connect you to someone else's dream?"

"I'm not buying it," Monique added. "It's way too convenient that everyone who can vouch for you is back at your crappy state school. Why not offer a sampler? Then we can decide whether or not you're legit."

Jamie shook her head, once. Her hair flowed as easily as water, and I hated her.

"My mother made me promise I wouldn't just give it away," she said. "Besides, it's for charity. The money is going to help cover my brother's medical bills."

Jamie's brother was apparently sick. Rumour had it that her mother was an archaeologist, or a lecturer, or something like that. She did a lot of work with ancient cultures and dead religions, and now Jamie was trying to sell us snake oil.

"At least let us see what it is," I said.

Monique nodded in agreement. "You can't make us buy something without seeing it first. That's like, against consumer law or something."

The other kids murmured in agreement. Jamie looked around, uncertain. She'd wanted a big crowd at lunch time, but now her audience—and potential buyers—were growing sour. A few teenagers peeled away to go and throw the footy. One dishevelled boy wandered off to take a nap.

The group dissolved after that, leaving Monique, Jamie,

and myself.

Monique and I had done this routine many times before. Whenever a hot new girl transferred to school, they usually needed to be taken down a notch. According to Monique, being the new student at school was a fertile opportunity. Many girls, who were popular at their old schools, tried to cement themselves as big players within their first week.

It had been a while since anyone tried to pull the 'exotic mystery' trick. The correct response to an exotic mystery scenario, we'd found, was to force the newcomer to show their hand as soon as possible. If they did, the mystery was gone, and things went back to the status quo. If the new arrival refused our offers to legitimise them, then they looked desperate for attention.

Two years ago, a new girl arrived at our school who claimed to read tarot cards. Monique and I had both sat down for public readings the day she arrived, and loudly declared all her mistakes about us, until she just gave up. I hear she's going to win the science award this year.

Monique gave me the signal, and we turned to leave.

"Wait, wait." Jamie reached for her satchel and held it close to her chest. "I'll let you have a quick look, but you can't touch it until you pay up. Promise."

We promised. Jamie then made us cross our hearts. We each drew a letter X over our white blouses, where we thought the heart must be.

"It's closer to the middle of your chest," Jamie corrected us. We did the gesture again. It felt strange doing the primary school ritual now that we were about to graduate, almost like we were performing our own off-brand mass.

"Satisfied?" Monique asked.

Jamie didn't answer, but she did open her satchel a crack, and leaned forward to let us peer inside. The gnats in the air left us alone then, and there was a great stillness to the air. Even the cicadas above us stopped screaming for a brief moment.

"I can't see," I complained, but then I saw them. Buried deep within the satchel, between some cheap aerosol deodorant and an emergency pad, there were two figurines. They were painted like the statues you can find in a miniature nativity scene. Their faces, however, resembled Lewis chessmen with bulging eyes and gnarled smiles.

"Where'd you get them?" I asked, suddenly intrigued. Monique glanced at me sideways, and I recomposed myself. "Not that we're going to pay for them."

Jamie shrugged. "That's a shame."

She zipped her satchel back up again. The darkness of the blue satchel swallowed those carved and terrible faces.

"I promised you a glimpse at the sleep idols, and now you've had a glimpse."

Luckily, the other students weren't nearby to witness the newcomer hold out the tantalising mystery: a mystery that I desperately wanted to unravel. Last month I'd put in my application for several history degrees at nearby universities, and I knew I'd never forgive myself if I didn't check the artefact out.

"Give us a moment," I said, and pulled Monique away.

We'd perfected the art of mumble gossip in the tenth grade. When I spoke, I would turn my back to the person we were talking about, in this case Jamie, so my voice didn't carry, and they couldn't read my lips. Monique would face the

126

person we were talking about, and make sure they didn't approach. When it was Monique's turn to speak, we would swap, and I would keep watch while Monique whispered into the wind.

"I want those statues," I said, facing the great juxtaposition that was the Arts and Sciences building. "I've never seen anything like them before, and if they can do what she claims..."

Monique faced the school, and I spun to eyeball Jamie. The new girl was picking the lint from her tartan skirt.

"Don't fall for it, Stacey," Monique chided me. "We just have to walk away and tell everyone she had two dusty bookends that she snatched from her mum's coffee table. Easy, problem solved."

We swapped directions again. "Or we could play along," I offered. "What if she finds someone else who rents them, and the power of suggestion causes them to believe it works? If we try it ourselves, then we can tell the whole grade that she's full of it."

Monique spun to face the school, and I spun to see Jamie now standing directly in front of me. I screamed, which caused Monique to jump as well.

"Have you come to a decision?" Jamie asked. She twirled her hair innocently. I had no idea how she'd managed to sneak up on us.

"When did you—?" Monique began to ask, but the bell rang, signalling the end of lunch.

I pulled out a crumpled twenty, and Monique sighed. She reached into her skirt pocket and matched it.

"Oh, you both want to pay?" Jamie asked. "I figured

Monique would want to have a go tonight and connect with me."

"Why would I want that?" Monique said with disgust.

"One for me, and one for Monique," I said. "Is that a problem?"

Jamie looked me up and down. Then she smiled. "Stacey, was it?"

"Yes."

She quickly took the cash, and then handed one idol to Monique, and one to me.

"Sweet dreams."

II

That night, I placed the figurine beneath my pillow before bed. The detailing on the statuette was exquisite, with spiralled patterns along its clothing. It felt surprisingly light. I tapped the sleep idol on its underside. It rang like wood, or perhaps bone.

Monique had taken the other statuette, which had resembled a mother suckling her child: her eyes bulging as though the baby was biting. I had opted for the figure of a young man who had a stomach-ache. He was hunched over. The space where his chin should have been was host to rows of tomb-like teeth that were twisted in agony.

Both of the figurines had been wrapped in a note, scratched out in flawless Queensland cursive, each letter desperately hugging the previous one, blurring together into the vague shapes of words that I recognised. The message was a blessing, and perhaps a vague promise of what the figurines were supposed to do:

May you and the one who holds the other statuette cleave.
May your love for each other be fixed,
With happiness garnished.
May you wear and weather true friendship.

I carefully lowered my pillow over the face of the sleep idol, and watched in morbid curiosity as his face was bisected by a line of crisp shadow. With the expression that had been etched on its face, it looked as though the small person was watching in terror as they were smothered.

On my bedside table, next to the rotary telephone dad let me use, there was a framed picture of Derek, Monique, and I at the sports carnival. Derek's arm disappeared behind my waist. Monique stood awkwardly beside me in that picture, caught off-guard by the photograph. I'd saved the photograph as soon as the film had been developed. Monique begged me to tear it up, because of how her face looks in it: her eyes are wide, almost like she's afraid of the camera. I refused to get rid of it though: I wanted to immortalise the way Derek looks at me in the photo.

I picked up the receiver for the telephone, and dialled Monique.

"Did you do it?" she asked.

"It's ready to go," I replied. "If this works, I call first dibs. I want to see if Derek and I can connect."

"If it works?" Monique scoffed. "That doesn't sound like you Stace. Since when did you start believing in this sort of stuff?"

"I dunno," I said. "I just feel good about it, that's all."

"Oh! Get a pen and paper ready," I said to Monique. "We can compare notes about how similar our dreams are."

We talked for an hour or so before bed. It was a routine that had been impressed upon our friendship since middle school. At the age of four my grandmother had died of a heart attack in front of me, and I'd struggled with night terrors ever since then. It was a struggle that had ended once Monique and I had quickly begun chatting at length every night before bed.

Initially, my parents weren't thrilled by the phone bill, or what they called an *extreme and troubling co-dependency*. Can't argue with the results though. After our nightly chat, my nightmares were a lot less terrible. So, dad bit the bullet and started working the weekend shift. I suspect back then he didn't relish the thought of his teenage daughter needing to sleep between mum and him.

"Goodnight," Monique said. She made two kissing noises like a Parisian.

III

My dream began as a scent. It was the smell of mum's flowers growing in the windowsills and in the garden outside: lavender, lupines, and snapdragons. The dream then became a sound. The sound of a cheap, loud pump trying and failing to clean a fish tank. Someone's dog was barking far away.

"Where are we?" Monique asked from somewhere nearby. "I can't see anything."

"My old home," I replied. The picture was blurry, but then it crystallised into clarity. "The house where Grandma died..."

"You don't have to talk about it."

"I loved it here, but we left. Moved to our current rental."

Monique gave a hefty sigh from beside me, but she was my mother. I'd forgotten how mum used to curl her fringe into a roll just above her eyebrows. I looked down at myself, and I was my own father back then: unkempt beard, and flannelette shirt tucked into acid-washed jeans.

"Who are you meant to be?" Monique asked, looking me up and down.

"My old man."

"Oh," Monique said, and quickly looked away with a blush.

We were in the living room. I'd forgotten about the stain on the carpet. Water had leaked from the roof a few years prior, and formed a stain on the floor in the perfect shape of Queensland. Dad had opted to leave it there.

"That's a lucky stain. It's one-in-a-million," I, my dad, said.

"We'll have to replace it before we sell," Monique, my mum, replied.

An enormous assortment of teddy bears, and other soft toys were strewn about the floor. We watched my past childhood self as she played on the floor. I was probably about four or five. A small doll was in my pudgy hands, and I was holding it in front of my face.

"What do you think she's doing?" Monique, my mother, asked.

"She's trying to cope, I suppose."

"Help! My heart!" the childhood version of me wrapped the doll's hands around its middle. "Stacey! Call the am-bu-wence. I'm dying! Stacey!" The doll fell on the ground, dead.

"Let's distract her with something else," Monique said.

"No, don't," I said quickly. "This is perfectly normal. She needs to try and understand what happened."

"Don't be ridiculous, this game is absolutely morbid," Monique said. She went over and swept me up. The child me grabbed her around the neck and sobbed uncontrollably.

"Stop crying," Monique said. "That's not helping anyone."

Mum stood there, holding me while she shook her head at my dad. Her rolled fringe bounced up and down.

"I really don't think that's best," I said, as my father. "If you keep coddling her like that, she isn't going to be able to cope with any sort of anxiety or trauma."

"What the hell would you know about what she's feeling?" Monique and my mum spat. She covered one of my young ears, not that it did anything. "She was my mother Harold. My mother died, and you've done nothing to help console me, or Stacey."

"I just don't know what to say."

I now realised we were parroting a conversation my parents had had a long time ago: a conversation that had been buried deep in my memory. I looked around again at my childhood home that I remembered so fondly. When I thought back to it, I usually just remembered the smells, the stain, the colour of the walls. What my dad saw was different. He saw the mortgage that this house still had on it. He saw the hundred thousand dollars we were going to lose, because I was too afraid to sleep again. The weight of all that money sat like an ulcer in his gut.

There was a knock at the door. I stood up.

"You get it," Monique said, forcing the head of my childhood self into the crook of her neck. My young me shook with the effort of crying.

"Can't you see I'm already doing that?" I felt the bitterness of the ulcer that my father must have felt. I opened the front door and stepped outside. There was no one there.

I looked up, and saw the bright white lights of stage lighting, and the deep shadows of blackout curtains behind them. The world outside was a cardboard cut-out. The houses across the street were merely facades: perfectly fine to look at through the living room window, but the illusion fell apart as soon as you saw them from a different angle.

"Who is it honey?" Monique called out in a strange voice. It sounded tense and unnatural, like she was remembering what to say.

I looked to the left and right. Students from our school were waiting in the stage wings. Their faces were shadows and fog: constantly shifting and uncertain. One of them, wearing a headset, leaned forward.

"There's no one here," she hissed at me.

"There's no one here," I said, louder than I needed to. I turned around and stepped back inside the house. Monique was herself again, but several years younger. Her hair was cut at that awful angle she had kept insisting was 'in'. She was no longer nursing me, but held a doll with an ease that felt unrealistic.

I was sweating under the intensity of the lights above us: yellows and whites. I closed the balsa wood door behind me, which had been painted to look like it was oak. A sea of faces that I didn't recognise were in front of us. Someone in the audience coughed.

"How strange, dear." Monique said, with an odd pause. "I was certain that I heard someone knocking."

A loud knocking sound reverberated throughout the arts centre.

"There it is! Again!" I found myself saying.

"Quick!" Monique said, turning back to the audience.

I stepped through the door again, and now I was somewhere different. I stood facing three mirrors in a changing room. Derek stood facing me in each of the mirrors, shirtless, and with his face caked in makeup. I looked down, and I was Derek. I was in a backstage changing room. The sound of applause died away.

"Derek!" I heard my voice call out.

I turned around. The changing room had a privacy curtain. I pulled it slightly to the side, and stuck just my head outside the curtain.

My younger self was standing outside, bashful, holding two wrapped boxes in front of her.

"Oh, hi there Stacey," I said to my younger, starry-eyed self. "Did you like the show?"

"You were amazing," my younger self said, and then quickly tried to backpedal. "The show was really clever."

"Yeah, um thanks I guess," Derek and I replied. I scratched the thin hair across my scalp, and was surprised by how nice it felt to have short hair. "Can I help you with anything, Stacey? You just aren't supposed to be back here."

"Oh, oh!" My younger self said. Her hand slapped herself in the mouth. She looked around at the other cast members removing their makeup, and hanging up costumes. The costumes were all neatly arrayed and labelled on portable clothes-racks throughout the changing rooms. Opening night.

"I'm sorry, I didn't realise I wasn't allowed here. I just came to bring you this." My younger self handed me a small box of chocolates. "It's to congratulate you on the show. I have one for Monique as well if you see her."

"Well, thanks for that," I said to Stacey. My younger self grinned like an idiot, and then bounced out of sight.

I pulled my head back through the changing curtain, and breathed a sigh of relief. "That was close."

Monique sat in her underwear, waiting on a stool in my changing room. She was trying to stifle her laughter.

"How cute," she said. "Stacey brought you chocolates."

"Yeah," Derek and I said with a shrug. He tossed the box on the floor near his shoes and shirt.

Monique crossed her arms. "Are you interested in Stacey?" she asked. "If you are, you better let me know sooner rather than later."

Derek shrugged. "She's nice I guess."

"But?"

"But she's not you," Derek and I said together.

Monique reached out towards me, but I forced myself to step back, breaking the scenario.

"What's wrong?" Monique asked, breaking character.

"How could you do this to me?" I asked. My voice strained to make itself heard through Derek's thicker vocal cords. "You were with Derek that night? You knew I liked him!"

Monique took another step towards me, and then froze. "Stacey? Is that you?"

There was a huge lump in my throat. I scrambled backwards, tripping over the curtain and ripping it from the railing. The other cast members turned to look at me, but their faces were vaporous, because I couldn't remember who they had been.

"Stacey!" Monique called out. She clutched her clothes to herself as she chased me out of the backstage area. "Stacey wait, it's not like that at all!"

I ran along the concrete hallway backstage, my footsteps echoing loudly as I ran past the stencilled signs that reminded me to be quiet. Several faceless people leered at me as I ran.

"Congratulations Derek!" one of them said.

"How are you feeling?" a taller one, perhaps a teacher,

asked me.

I ran past the ropes and rigging behind the stage, Monique's feet slapped at the concrete behind me.

"Wait Stacey!" Monique yelled. Her voice was hoarse.

I saw the fire exit at the rear of the stage. A long black bar across it that begged to be pushed. I reached it, and heaved against it, but the door remained shut.

"No," I gasped, and pushed against it again. I couldn't bear the thought of hearing Monique talk about her and Derek. I clutched my stomach, and felt as though I was going to vomit.

"Stacey," Monique said, coughing and trying to talk through a lump of phlegm in her throat.

Monique stood. Her costume clutched to her chest like it was a babe. Her eyes were wide and disbelieving. Monique was a bone statue of a mother and her child, a living copy of the figurine that was currently buried beneath her pillow. I grabbed my gut as I felt the pain of her betrayal deep, deep within me. I felt my skin calcify, and knew that I too must resemble the statuette beneath my head.

Monique watched me, horrified, and then let out a metallic scream—which turned out to be my alarm clock.

I sat bolt upright in bed, and slammed my hand onto the clock to silence the bells. I was even more tired than before I went to bed. I lifted my pillow, and saw that the figurine had changed.

IV

I tried to avoid Monique at school, even going so far as to eat my lunch in a bathroom stall. I don't think I'd ever been forced to eat in a stall before. In fact, I usually went out of my way to oust anyone who I found being a loner in here.

Toilet lunches are terrible. The door would slam open every few minutes, heralding the arrival of a group of giggling girls. This would usually be followed by several rather unappetising sounds, and then the running of tap water, the slam of the door again, and silence.

Dad had packed sandwiches today: butter with jam. I hated butter, and he knew it. I looked down at the soggy bite I'd taken from the white bread, and felt myself tearing up again.

The door slammed open, and then closed. No giggling.

I waited, but there were no other noises. Underneath the stall's door, I saw two polished leather shoes, filled with thin ankles in black stockings. The two feet turned away from me, and there was a thud as something leaned against the toilet door. Someone knocked, twice.

"Occupied," I said quietly.

There was a pause, and then Monique's face appeared upside-down, grinning maniacally.

"Found you!" she sang.

She crawled under the stall door and stood in front of me. Monique had always been tall for a girl. Her curly hair was a frizzy halo around her face, and she towered over me as I sat on my porcelain throne.

"What are you doing here?" Monique asked. The wide grin hadn't left her face.

"Leave me alone."

Monique sniffed the air, twice. "Do you want to talk about last night?"

"I want to be alone."

She shrugged, and then squatted on the wet, tiled floor in front of me. "We might as well talk it through then. What did you dream about?"

"I saw you with Derek, the night of the Year Ten drama."

Monique nodded. "Yeah, I remember that."

"Are you going to apologise?"

Monique laughed lightly, and blew a ringlet of hair that had fallen in front of her eyes. "For what Stacey? For a dream? I wasn't in control of what happened. Neither of us were. I don't know why my dream was about Derek."

"Deep down inside, you must like him," I said, trying not to pout. "Why else would you have a dream about being with him?"

Monique made a face. "I don't know what to tell you Stacey. It wasn't on purpose. I'm sure you probably didn't want to dream about your parents fighting either. Besides, you're missing the bigger picture."

"What's that?"

"The bigger picture is that Jamie was right about our

dreams connecting, and I hate that. Both of the dreams were unpleasant. It wasn't exactly the power trip she was selling to everyone yesterday."

I swallowed the lump in my throat, and the pain in my gut began to subside. "Yeah, I guess so."

"Did you bring your figurine?"

I nodded. My satchel was tucked beside the toilet, and I retrieved the sleep idol from it. Monique reached into her bag also, and produced hers. As I suspected, her figurine had changed as well.

"Well, look-it-that," Monique said.

The two statues were of a man and a woman once again.

"What's your figurine supposed to be?" I asked.

Monique's statuette was a man folded in half, like a piece of paper, straight through the heart. His face was now positioned to stare cleanly into his own belly button. His arms were dislocated, and twisted backwards.

My statuette depicted a female figure, reclining under a light blanket, which had been tastefully draped to conceal her body. The blanket also wrapped up and over the statuette's head, however, blinding it. It's teeth and mouth were trying to bite through the fabric.

We held the two figurines together, and their bodies fit each other like a jigsaw. It looked as though both figurines were straining to reach out and embrace each other.

"They give me the willies," I said.

"We shouldn't use them again," Monique replied. "Maybe we could burn them, or bury them somewhere."

"I've got a good backyard," I offered. "I can bury them out behind the shed where no one will find them."

Monique gave me her figurine, and I placed them both in my satchel.

"I'm sorry again about what happened in the dream," Monique said. "I wasn't really in control of what I was doing, until you broke the spell and started running."

I stood up, and we embraced each other. Monique turned the latch and unlocked the stall.

We found Jamie at the undercover area before lunch concluded. She was sitting at a table packed with senior boys. Her fake eyelashes were closed in concentration. Her orange, chemically-tanned hands were tracing circles in Derek's palm.

"What the hell do you think you're doing?" I asked.

"It's fine," Derek said with a smirk. "She's just reading my future."

Jamie's eyelids fluttered dramatically. She spoke in a breathy voice that reverberated across the concrete. "Yes, yes. I see a new relationship in your future Derek. Someone very close to you will leave your life, and a mysterious stranger will fill the space left behind." Her painted fingertips lingered on Derek's love line for a moment longer. She gasped. "Oh my."

"Holy Virgin Mary," Monique swore.

I had stopped processing what was happening as soon as I realised Jamie was touching Derek. The boy had a dumb grin on his face. He was nodding to whatever Jamie was excreting from her mouth.

I had grabbed Jamie by her hair before I realised what I was doing. There was a maintenance shed at the corner of the undercover area. I yanked her towards it.

"Let's go."

"Woah, woah Stacey!" Derek yelled. His eyes were wide.

"Just a moment dear," I said, pulling Jamie along like a good little dog.

"Quick, get a teacher!" one of the senior boys shouted.

Two grade elevens were holding hands behind the maintenance shed. They saw me coming, and must have realised I didn't care about who had booked the space, because they quickly scrambled out of my way.

Once we were out of eyesight, Monique grabbed one of Jamie's fake fingernails.

"What a cute colour," she said.

There was a loud crack, and Jamie screamed as Monique snapped off one of her nails. Monique reached up a hand to slap Jamie across the face, but I stopped her.

"We don't want the teachers to see a bruise."

Jamie cowered, gripping her index finger so tightly it was turning purple. Monique backed me up. She stuck her foot up against the shed at waist height, preventing Jamie from escaping.

"We don't have much time," I explained through the crimson that was clouding my vision. "So, I want to make it perfectly abundant to you that if you ever speak to Derek again, I'll cut you so that no boy ever looks at you again."

Jamie nodded. She was biting her lip so hard that a thin trickle of red ran down her chin. Monique could smell the blood, like a shark. Her eyes were rolling in her skull with pure delight.

"Oh, and your stupid statues didn't do a damned thing."

"That's false advertising," Monique chimed in.

"You could go to jail for swindling us. It's practically stealing."

"My mum's a barrister," Monique said, leaning close to the terrified Jamie. "She could really mess up your family for selling us dodgy merchandise."

"My dad's the chair of the PT committee," I added. "You'll probably get expelled for being such a bad influence."

"Not to mention all this witchcraft," Monique said, she was eyeing the other fingernails with a glint in her eyes. "Can you imagine how Sister Fourie will respond when she finds out about palm reading in her school? You practically sold us voodoo dolls. You'd get expelled for sure, so you're lucky we're going to burn those figurines instead."

Jamie's eyes widened, and she shook her head quickly. "No, please you can't. My brother would be devastated if you destroyed them. Besides, someone already tried to do that and then..."

Monique snapped off a fake thumbnail. I bet Armstrong heard it from the moon.

Jamie screamed, back arching. She collapsed, exhausted and wretched. Her mascara was ruined in two terrible black lines down her face. There was a commotion on the other side of the shed. When Mr Reynolds rounded the corner with Derek and several other boys in tow, Monique and I were tenderly embracing Jamie and crying as well.

"What's going on here girls? You're out of bounds."

"Sir," Monique cried tears that had been perfectly honed through years of drama class. She grabbed Mr Reynold's hand, tightly, and blew a strand of hair out of her face. "Jamie broke her nails and it looks so horrible and we were mad at her but she's hurt herself so badly that we can't be angry at her anymore and I'm sorry that we're out of bounds but we wanted to talk to her about some things she said that were concerning us but now—"

"—Alright, um, that's okay." Mr Reynolds said, uncertainly. Everyone present could see he was acutely aware of Monique's grasp of his hand. "Let's get her to sickbay."

"Sir, they were going to kill her!" said one of the senior boys in disbelief.

"Are you okay, Jamie, is it?" Mr Reynolds asked. He tried to get a good look at Jamie's face, but Monique shook her head, gently placing her own cheek over Jamie's protectively.

"I'm fine," Jamie said softly. "We had an argument, and I broke my nails accidentally."

"Well, you heard her." Mr Reynolds said, dropping the case. "Come along Jamie, let's get you to the health bay. Monique, maybe you could come along as well, just so she has a friend."

"Of course!" Monique said, wiping her eyes.

The senior boys were complaining loudly until Jamie was out of sight.

"Alright, listen up," I said to them. "Two of you have girlfriends who I'm on good terms with. If you go spreading gossip about Monique and I, then I'll tell them exactly what I saw: a group of hormone-addled boys gleefully getting their palms read, just as an excuse to hold hands with the new girl."

Two of the boys walked away immediately. Derek was frowning, but I was saving him for last. I turned to the other senior boy there. He inhaled sharply when I looked at him.

"Tom, I know you don't have a girlfriend, so you might be thinking you can go all White Knight and defend Jamie's honour, or something creepy."

From the deflated look on his face, that had been exactly what he was planning.

"Let me be the first to advise you against that. For one, I've never seen it work. Jamie's the sort of person who will use others to get what she wants. She's even stolen money from Monique and me. Are you sure you want to get involved in that?"

Tom shrivelled up.

"Besides," I added. "Monique is currently single, and she thinks you're cute. You'll have a much better year if you try getting to know her, instead."

Tom didn't look uncertain anymore. He smiled apologetically at Derek, and wandered off to contemplate his future. Monique had never said anything about Tom, but we knew the routine well by now. She would play along for a week or two, until Tom forgot about the incident.

That left Derek.

My orange hair had become a mess during all the excitement. I began to curl it around a manicured finger, so I didn't have to look at him. "Derek, how could you do that to me?"

He looked at his feet. "It didn't mean anything Stacey. We were just having fun."

"It looked like you were having a little too much fun Derek. I love you, and it made me so mad seeing her with you, like that."

There was something in the dirt, and Derek kicked it lightly. "I didn't realise you'd be mad."

"I could've gotten in a lot of trouble because of your friends. I'm not lying Derek, that girl is bad news. Took forty bucks from Monique and I."

"What'd she do? Pinch it out of your purses?"

"I'll tell you another time. Right now, I need some space."

"Okay," Derek squeezed my hand. "I'm sorry."

"I forgive you. Please, just think about my feelings next time."

V

That evening, I carefully dug a shallow grave for the statuettes behind my father's shed. The shed was positioned in the left-hand pocket of the yard, beneath an old tree that refused to die, no matter how many times dad laced the ground with poison.

Dad had been promising me he'd do some gardening out here for the past three years. His shovel and pick had been left out in the elements as proof that he'd get around to it, and now they were rusted. I used the splintering shovel to pat down the soft mound of dirt that covered where the statuettes lay.

"Did you do it?" Monique asked me that night, over the wire.

"Of course," I answered. "Piece of cake."

"Tom called me earlier," Monique said with a sigh.

"Aww, that's sweet."

"He's gone all mushy about his feelings, and how it's his destiny to be with me."

"Well, it could be worse. Remember when I pretended to like Richard Smith last year?"

"Eww!" came the scream of disgust from Monique. I could hear her dry-heaving. "The boy who thought he was a wizard?"

"See? At least Tom doesn't have pustules on his lips."

"Whatever happened to Richard anyway?" Monique asked.

"You didn't hear? His mum confronted the PT committee and claimed that my breakup with him was *unabashedly public, and frankly quite psychotic*. He quit to go get home-schooled the next day."

"Didn't he have a sister or something?"

"A twin sister, non-identical. He used to brag about how hot she was, and how much I reminded him of her. It was rather unpleasant."

"Well, at least they'll be happy together. Two weirdo twins getting home-schooled."

"I don't think she was home-schooled," I said, dredging up some unpleasant conversations I'd had while staring at Richard Smith's swollen pus sacks. "He left his previous school because he was bullied, but I reckon she stayed there."

"Can we stop talking about Richard, please?" Monique whined. "I can remember his skin oozing."

That night we didn't talk as long as we usually would. My exhaustion from the previous night was starting to get to me. After we hung up, I lay completely still on my pastel sheets, as my bedroom spun around me. My room was immense. Mum had decided long ago that I'd sleep better in the master bedroom. My parents had taken the smaller one down the hall. That was a long time ago.

There was a gentle knock on my door.

"Yeah?" I called out. The door cracked open slightly, and my father stuck his head through.

"Hey princess," he whispered through the crack. "How was your day?"

"Exhausting. I can't really talk about it."

Dad yawned, and rubbed the dark circles under his eyes.

"I heard you scream last night. Do you want the night light back on?"

"Yeah."

Dad turned off the ceiling light, and bent down to plug a small unicorn lamp into the wall. The room was filled with colourful splotches of soft light.

"You call out if you need anything from your old man."

"You got it."

The man who was my father, the man who I had been last night, closed the door behind him. I remembered the steady pain of an ulcer, and I winced.

VI

I awoke suddenly, coddled in my blankets. It was still dark outside. The night light spun a carousel of soft green light across my bedroom. There was a gentle knock at the door.

"Come in."

My father poked his head through the doorway once again. His face was smoother than it had been earlier, but also sadder.

"Hey princess, I need to have a quick talk with you."

I sat up in bed, and pulled the sheets around me. The night was unusually cold for August. Dad lowered himself down to sit on the edge of the mattress. He moved like he was a hundred years old.

"Sweetie, your mum and I have been talking," he began. In the darkness, I heard the sharp exhale of his breath.

"Is mum okay?" I asked. "I didn't hear her yelling tonight."

"Your mum needed a holiday," dad replied. He leaned back, and I saw his face silhouetted in the thin crack of light from the door. "I shouldn't have woken you up. Get some sleep and I'll talk to you tomorrow."

"She's gone, hasn't she?" I asked.

I heard a few choked sobs, and ragged breathing between them.

"It's just a holiday," he lied. "She'll be back kiddo, you'll see."

I rested a tiny hand on my father's shoulder and shook my head. He probably couldn't see the stern look that I gave him.

"We both know that isn't true," I replied. "There's no sense in lying about it father."

"Why am I back here?" Monique asked from inside my father.

"I don't know."

"Did he really tell you about the separation in the middle of the night like this?"

"I think so. I can't really remember," I replied. "I never saw what he looked like while he cried."

"Our dreams seem very reliant on what we did and didn't notice back then," my father and Monique said.

We let the moment hang heavily in the air between us.

"I didn't realise you were so young when they split," Monique said.

"I was pretending to be brave, but I think it ended up hurting dad more. His life fell apart, and here was his holier-than-thou daughter, lecturing him on how separation works. I think I damaged our relationship that night."

"Maybe."

"I think I did." I wiped a tear from my cheek.

The door opened a crack. I saw my mother standing there, where she shouldn't have been. She was outlined in the doorway: a thin template of orange light in the shape of my childhood mother. At the edges of her face, the light crept along her cheeks a little further. She was grinning.

"Mum?" I asked.

Monique, my father, turned and saw my mother standing there.

"Was she listening that night?" Monique asked.

"No, she'd already left."

"Do you want to come in, Mrs Thompson?" Monique asked.

"No, don't invite her inside!"

It was too late, however. The doorway opened wider, and my mother stepped into the room. The door slammed shut behind her.

Monique-inside-my-father edged closer to me. "Why isn't she talking?"

I could barely see where my mother was. The night light wasn't casting any actual illumination throughout the room. However, I could see a dark space missing along the walls, blocked by the body of my mother.

"Turn the big light on," I said, heart pounding. "Turn it on quickly."

"You turn it on," Monique said. "I'm not moving."

I estimated where my mother was. Perhaps in the middle of the room, between us and the light switch next to the door. I stood up on my mattress, legs shaking. The springs sounded like metallic screams.

"You need to distract mum," I said to Monique. "She'll get me if I go for the switch."

"Dream on," Monique said. "You fight your creepy mum all by yourself."

I made a dash for it. My feet sank into the mattress deeply as I began the run-up. Each step was accompanied by a metallic screech, signalling where I was.

As I leapt, my foot snagged the railing at the end of my bed, and I cursed myself. I'd forgotten about the ornate trappings of the pink princess bed that I'd begged dad to buy me. I hit the ground, and it felt like I'd had my leg chopped off at the shin.

I could feel my mother breathing over me as I scrambled on hands and knees past her. At that moment I remembered a long-forgotten terror that I had always known: my mother could see in the dark far better than I could.

Her arms encircled me like cold, wet serpents.

I screamed, and Monique did as well. The balls of colour from the little unicorn night light began to throb like a heartbeat across the walls and surfaces around us. I heard the sound of ripping fabric, and I felt my mother begin to swaddle me in strips from my bedsheets. Her grip was impossibly strong, as I tried and failed to kick at her. Monique was pressed flat against the wall, splotches of colour from the night light washed across her dimly. My legs were now bound by the sheets, and I heard the sound of children laughing cruelly.

"Monique!" I begged. "Monique, please, you have to turn the light on."

My feet were lifted high above my head, and the wrapping continued with spider-like efficiency. Next, my chest and abdomen were constricted, as the bedsheets squeezed my ribs closer together.

"Monique," I gasped, struggling to find enough air to speak.

My mother, sensing Monique, looked up in time to see her leap over the bed railing. The sounds of laughing and jeering became louder and louder as Monique tried to reach the door.

The shape of my mother lunged at the shadow of my friend. There was the sound of something ripping, and then there was a loud crack as the light switch was thrown.

The sound of children laughing was now deafening. I was standing behind the school cafeteria, in a thick crowd of blurry faces. I could see Richard's face clearly, however. It was covered in spots and pus. He was reaching out to try and lead me away from the group.

"Don't touch me Richard, you piece of garbage," I said. "I've sat on toilet seats that were cleaner than your face, and I've been to Splendour in the Grass."

Richard recoiled as the crowd laughed again. His eyes scanned for a friendly face among his year level, but there weren't any. Richard turned back to me, pleading.

"Give me another chance. I won't pick at my skin anymore."

The constable's daughter covered her mouth to hide her laughter. Richard had sat next to her each week in biology, and picked holes in his face whenever they'd done lab work.

"Richard, just the thought of you touching me with your fetid body fluids makes me want to study abroad."

"Stop talking about my skin!"

To his credit, Richard hadn't burst into tears yet. He was still trying to talk me down from the break-up. "You agreed to go out with me, so what changed?"

"I only agreed to go out with you because I felt sorry for you," I lied. In reality, Monique and I had desperately needed cash to go shopping through the summer catalogue. Having a boyfriend makes sound fiscal sense: you can significantly cut costs on things like swimsuits and underwear.

"You hadn't made any friends, and I felt bad. That's the only reason I decided to go out with you, because I wanted you to fit in."

His bottom lip began to quiver.

"I thought you might be a really nice guy on the inside, you know. Like a frog prince or something—"

Monique cackled from the edge of the crowd.

"—but it has dawned on me, with a sudden and unquenchable terror, that you are perhaps the most boring boy I've ever spoken to."

A tear welled up in Richard's eye without warning, hanging there like a white flag.

"You said you liked talking about spells and incantations with me. We were going to make a love potion."

"Richard, I can't keep repeating myself like this," I said. "Please, stop making a scene in front of all my friends." In my periphery, I could see that Monique was standing next to Derek. She'd brought him to the conclusion of the proceedings: when I would look saintly. "I said a lot of things to try and make you feel better about yourself." I dropped my eyes and played with the hem of my skirt. "I mean, you kept insisting for other things too, but I just couldn't bring myself—"

"You piece of scum!" yelled one of the blurry senior boys. He threw his apple core at Richard and it bounced off his cheap shoe. I couldn't identify the senior. One of my not-so-secret admirers, perhaps. "Stacey's an angel. You better not have forced yourself on her."

"What?" Richard's head shook, uncomprehending. His voice was soft. "No, I didn't do anything like that."

"Richard, I'm sorry, I'm just saving myself for someone special," and here I made sure I locked eyes with Derek.

It was my second time living through the events of that day. That might be why I noticed something strange about how Monique and Derek were standing. Monique's face was foggy, like the others in the crowd. Derek's face, on the other hand, was crystal clear. Judging by his shoulder, it looked as though Derek's arm was stretched out at a strange angle.

I shook the thought away, and spun around to confront Richard. I could see the pieces falling into place. He could sense it too, like a dog hearing thunder: another school where he would be forced to camouflage himself. Eating alone in dark corners of the schoolyard to avoid the scorn of other students.

Desperation can make people do funny things.

Richard was now exposed to a spotlight he wasn't designed to inhabit. He could try and plead his innocence, which might work, but I was anticipating a teacher to round the corner any moment and bring the whole thing to a climactic end. Alternatively, he could run away, which would be an admission of guilt on his part.

I played a lot of chess with my father growing up. Whenever he started talking about my mother and the divorce, I'd suggest a game. As a result, I'd won the middle school tournament three times in a row. Pinning, forking, and skewering are all tactics I'm intimately familiar with. You give your opponent two choices: both are terrible, and both choices benefit you. Richard, on the other hand, decided to knock over his king.

He stood, quivering, as he realised what I was saying, and how it was going to affect all of the friendships he thought he'd made. He charged towards Monique, who was hurling insults above all the other voices in the crowd. His hand rose up to strike her cloudy face, but he hesitated.

I watched as Derek sank his fist into Richard's abdomen. I heard the loud sound of air escaping, and then Richard was on the floor. A foot from someone else kicked him in the back sharply. Richard lay curled up. Someone grabbed his arm and bent it sharply behind his back, landing a heel into Richard's side. I heard something snap. Richard's other arm was wrenched backwards, to force him upright. He was roughly marched away by three seniors.

"Stacey!" Richard yelled. "Stacey, it's me!"

The words confused me for a moment, but then I looked back at the Monique, standing next to Derek. She stood just as vacantly as the rest of the crowd. I reached out and took her hand, but it felt cold.

I pulled away from her. She was like a faceless mannequin, disinterested in her surroundings now that the dream sequence was over. Derek, however, was watching me closely. His hand was firmly planted on Monique's butt.

"What are you doing that for?" I asked.

"To be honest, I don't know." Derek replied. "I'm just living out your memory, or Monique's memory, and this is what happened."

"Who are you?" I asked.

"I'm not sure." Derek said, with a warm smile that was very familiar to me. His dark brown eyes were twisted and cruel as he looked at me. "Who do I look like to you?"

Derek picked up the mannequin of Monique, and tucked her under his arm. The stage spotlight swung from me, onto him. He set off towards stage right, carrying the husk of my friend's body with him. The audience stood and applauded in unison.

"Wait, where are you going?" I shouted over the raucous.

"I want to find a mirror," Derek called back. "I'm curious."

As Derek made his way backstage, I looked around at the silhouettes and shadows of my classmates, who were lined up to bow and curtsy at the audience. The constable's daughter noticed my hesitation, mid-curtsy.

"How's our patient today?" she asked in a deep man's voice. "Ah, Jim? We'll have to get this one cleaned up."

I ran to catch Derek. He was taking big strides across the stage, which had been dressed to look like our schoolyard. He stepped behind the curtain wings, and made his way along the concrete hallway backstage. He reached the changing rooms, and switched the lights on with Monique's foot.

The backstage changing rooms were deserted. I hung back at the doorway, panting. Derek had his eyes closed. He suddenly remembered he was carrying Monique, and carefully propped her up against the wall. Then he took a deep breath, and jumped in front of the warmly-lit makeup mirrors. I watched as he stared at his own face, examining it from several different angles.

"Where's Monique?" I asked.

Distracted, Derek motioned to the husk that was leaning near the fire extinguisher.

"No, the real Monique," I said.

Derek didn't reply. He pressed his nose to the glass of the mirror. A small murmur escaped his throat, like the cry of a kitten. Then he began to laugh a long, terrible laugh that echoed through the change rooms, and reverberated out across the empty stage behind us. It was a deep and unpleasant sound that lasted far too long. He stood there, heaving in air so that he could continue to laugh. Spittle landed on his own reflection as he watched himself, unblinking. His laugh softened into a slow, rhythmic breathing.

"Derek?" he asked. He looked at me through his reflection, and they both seemed to be shouting. Both Derek and his reflection stared at me with furious expressions. "Do you know the disgusting things he said about you? Do you have any idea how little he respects you? To him, you're a pretty plaything he can throw away once he graduates—"

"—Listen," I took a deep breath, and tried to regain my composure. "I don't know who you are, or why you're here in my dream—"

Derek's reflection burst into laughter, but Derek held up a hand to stop it.

"You're very much mistaken," Derek said. He took a slow step towards me. A very precise movement, dividing the space between us by exactly a third. "You had your dream earlier tonight."

I took a step backwards, but Monique's husk was behind me, blocking my retreat.

Derek took another step forward, dividing the distance between us again, so that just one third remained.

"We're in my dream right now Stacey," Derek said. He licked his full lips as he approached. "I've had this dream every night. It's the only dream I can remember. I know it very well. I know where the cracks and the seams are. I know which threads I can unravel to try and steer it, and which threads I must never, ever touch."

He took his final step towards me. Our toes were touching, and my nose was level with his chest.

Why, oh why, do I always like tall boys?

"I want to wake up now," I said with a pain in my throat.

The circumference of Derek's face was illuminated by the warm lighting behind him.

"Of course," Derek said. "You've got a big day tomorrow, I'm sure. We'll continue our chat tomorrow night."

He reached over me, and picked up Monique's husk, which suddenly began to scream.

VII

Dad found me in the backyard at six o'clock in the morning, hefting the shovel and trying to unearth the sleep idols from where I'd buried them.

"Come back inside this instant," he said. "You're going to get sick out here."

My silk boxer shorts were covered in mud, and my legs were slick with dew. I could feel myself swaying as I stood in the cold morning air.

"You look like you haven't slept in a week," dad said. He touched my forehead gingerly. "You should stay home and get some rest."

I continued digging. "I have to speak to someone at school today. It's urgent."

The shovel smacked against something solid, and I pried the statuette from the mud with shivering arms.

"Sweetie," dad put his jacket around me, "come inside."

No amount of pleading would make me stay at home. I didn't want to drift off to sleep, and be confronted by whoever was controlling Derek in my dreams. I also needed to confront Jamie about the sleep idols.

Dad rinsed the statuettes off in the sink while I washed my

face and got dressed. In the mirror, my eyes were sunken and bloodshot. My hair was oily and tangled, but I didn't bother brushing it.

"What are these things?" Dad asked when I collected my satchel from the kitchen table. From the smell of bacon and eggs, he was making breakfast to cheer me up.

"These figurines?" I asked, examining them closely. "They're the latest thing. Collectable and tradeable. Like Pokémon cards."

I no longer knew which statuette represented me, and which one represented Monique. They'd changed again in the night. One statuette reclined on its back, but the figure had almost been sawn in half.

The other figure was of a young girl as well. This one slept peacefully because she'd been lobotomised. Her head was cut in a perfect circle above the eyebrows. Instead of her brain, a pair of eyes peered out from her cranial cavity.

"They're a bit bulky, aren't they?" Dad asked from the stovetop. "Not to mention morbid. How many are there to collect?"

I flinched. "That's a very good question."

I waited at the school's front gate for fifteen minutes, but Monique didn't show up. Derek spotted me and wandered up.

"Hey babe." He planted a kiss on my cheek, despite the teacher on duty being a few metres away. "You look like crap."

I wiped my eyes. They felt puffy. "Tell me what you dreamed about last night."

"Oh," he leaned back, assessing me. "Why?"

"Yes," I grabbed the hem of his shirt. "Tell me now."

"Is this a trick?"

"Tell me."

Derek squinted his eyes, assessing me. Then he smiled, and his eyes glazed over stupidly. "I dreamt about the girls' volleyball team."

The whole school heard the insults that I hurled at Derek's back, as he drifted towards the basketball courts. When I finally caught my breath, however, Monique still hadn't arrived.

I decided to confront Jamie by myself.

I found her behind the Arts and Sciences building, practising her henna tattoos on a banana. She stood up as I approached.

"Pax?" I asked.

"What?"

"I want a ceasefire. Let's talk about things." I pulled a small vial of neon blue nail polish from my satchel, and handed it to her. Jamie took it, somewhat reluctantly, and gestured to the bench she had been sitting on.

"Okay, I guess I can spare a moment."

I pulled out the sleep idols, and placed them on the bench between us.

"I thought you burnt them?" she asked. Her eyes narrowed.

"I buried them instead," I replied. "Here's the problem, however: Monique and I are still connected in dreamland."

Jamie looked at me like I was unstable. "That's not the way they work. You pay me, use them for a night, and then you're *supposed* to return them."

"How many statuettes are there?" I asked flatly.

"Two," Jamie replied. She glanced over her shoulder,

probably calculating her chances of making a get-away.

"I know you've got one Jamie, or you gave a third one to some crazy person who has decided to stalk me."

Jamie's fists clenched tightly.

"There's just two statuettes, you psycho. Richard only made two."

As soon as the words had escaped, Jamie slapped her hands over her mouth, desperately trying to force the words back inside. Two pink band-aids were coiled around the purple, fleshy skin where her fingernails used to be.

"Richard?" I asked. "Richard Smith?"

Jamie shook her head, mouth firmly covered by her hands.

"I dreamt about Richard last night," I admitted.

Jamie cautiously lowered her hands. "You did?"

"We used to date."

Jamie looked across the oval, at the shaded spot where she'd sold us the figurines. "I know."

"Are you his friend?" I asked. "Girlfriend?"

"His twin," she corrected. "Non-identical."

"So, what's the game here, exactly?"

Jamie sighed, and then she began to cry quietly. I dug a tissue out of my satchel.

"Here."

"Richard got bullied a lot."

"I know."

"It started at our previous school. They changed him. Turned him inside-out with anxiety. Dad took him to two self-defence classes before Richard gave up. Then he became obsessed with spells, and supernatural protection."

"He thought he was a wizard."

Jamie shook her head. "No, he was just very, very scared. He needed to believe that something more powerful than his teachers, or the school system, would be willing to protect him."

I looked down at the statuettes between us, and their disfigured bodies. Something icy gripped my spine.

"It went too far."

"I guess it did," Jamie agreed. "He dug up the remains of our old Labrador. I didn't know about that until much later, of course. He carved those idols from the bones."

I inched further away from the figurines.

"He used to sit in his room every day after school, for months, and whisper his hatred to those figurines. Used to write spells for them too."

We sat in silence as the footy boys ran past, puffing vapour into the cold air as they jogged.

"Then what?" I prodded, once the last pair of tiny shorts had disappeared around the corner.

"They didn't work. He was hospitalised one day, after the boys were particularly rough with him."

"You didn't try and stop things?"

The tears fell in a cascade down Jamie's cheeks. Unlike me, she was beautiful when she cried. It made me hate her even more.

"Why do you think I spend my time trying to earn money for his treatment? I've felt so guilty about this, for so long. He gave up talking to the teachers. They didn't believe him anyway. A few of the really clever boys were the ringleaders. He didn't tell the police anything, either. So, Mum and dad pulled him out of school. He still believed in the magic of those statuettes, though. I saw him in bed, cuddling them for protection. I thought he'd give up on the whole thing, but he didn't. He doubled down on it. Then one day he just sat me down, and told me that I should rent the figurines out."

"And you did? You hawked the statuettes at your old school as well?" I asked.

Jamie nodded. "It was a big school. Very few people knew that Richard and I were siblings. We don't look anything alike." The sun made Jamie's smooth cheeks flush a light pink. The wind stirred her long, blonde hair.

"You can say that again."

"I didn't really understand what was happening, but I figured I'd do it, if it made him feel better."

Jamie dug around in her school satchel for a moment, and produced a crumpled piece of paper. She handed it to me. The paper was a shopping list of names, with most of them crossed off. Most of the names I didn't know.

"Richard had a list of people he wanted me to give the idols to. All his old bullies, or people close to them. So, I made some promises, like: 'you can use these to visit me in your dreams, if you like. Just twenty bucks.' I managed to rent them to every guy on that list within a month. They always returned them, and thanked me profusely. I thought it was just the power of suggestion, you know. They thought about it so much, that they imagined it had worked."

Half-way down the list, the colour of the pen changed. I recognised these names. A few of them had been big admirers of mine, who had intervened when Richard threatened Monique. I saw Tom's name on the list, as well as two other boys that were with Derek when their palms were being read.

At the bottom of the list, I saw Monique's next to Derek's name. Both were written in capitals, and had been circled several times with thick ink for emphasis. Out of the corner of my eye, I could see her glancing between the statuettes and me.

"What happens to those people who use the statues?" I asked.

"Nothing," Jamie replied. "Well...occasionally people approach me, and ask some questions. Those boys at the top of the list just stopped coming to school. I didn't really notice though. It was a big school. People transfer away all the time, don't they? Some of them got sick, I heard. Some of them just needed time away. They were probably stressed from schoolwork. That must have been it."

"Why do you think Richard wrote this list of names for you, if the idols don't do anything?"

Jamie made a pouting face as she thought. "I'm not sure. It must have been important to him for some reason. Perhaps it was a list of people who could be helped by the figurines? Richard was always looking out for people."

I searched for a trace of sarcasm or dishonesty on Jamie's face, but I could tell that she now believed her own lie.

"You've never used the sleep idols yourself then? You've always just pretended that you would?"

"That's right. I've never used them."

"Why?"

"Because I know it's not real, Stacey. It made Richard happy, and that was enough. Whenever I told him that I'd sold the statues to someone else on the list, he'd smile this big grin. I hadn't seen him smile like that since we were kids, you know. Now it helps pay for his treatment, and that makes my mother happy. I'm not hurting anybody, so who cares?"

"Why'd Richard end up coming here then?" I asked.

Jamie wiped away a tear with the tissue I'd given her.

"Mum couldn't cope with Richard around the house. His spells and potions became more and more...disturbing. So, she sent him here to Catholic school to try and straighten him out. Then you happened to him, Stacey. He met you, and then suddenly he asked me to stop using the idols. Mum thought it was a genuine miracle."

I felt a pang of regret in the pit of my stomach.

"He'd never had a girl take a second look at him. After you two started dating, he put the statuettes away in a shoebox. I thought that was the end of it. Then things got more hectic at my school. My boyfriend broke up with me, when he heard about the deals I was supposedly making with old boys at school. To my horror, someone dobbed on me. Told my mum that I was being friendly with Richard's old bullies. She home-schooled me after that."

"Probably a good thing. You would've looked like a witch, with all those boys disappearing."

Jamie stood and turned on me. Stance wide.

"The only witch here is you, Stacey. Did you know Richard stole cash from our mum's purse to try and buy you nice things? I heard the beatings dad gave Richard when he found out, but Richard kept taking the money to make you happy. Then you ripped my brother's heart out in public. You poked around in his self-esteem like a Jenga tower, and then you pulled on the right tile to break him."

She pointed at the list in my hands. "Monique and Derek got added to that list of bullies right before Richard got sick.

169

Turn the paper over."

I did. On the other side, a name was written: *Stacey Smith*. My name and his name. A love heart was carved into the paper roughly, and the page had ripped. Then the name again: Stacey Smith. Then another heart that had been drawn so vigorously that it tore the paper. The back of the page was covered.

I jumped up, disgusted, and met Jamie at eye level. It was probably too sudden. My head swam, and I realised I desperately needed sleep.

"Your brother is a creep, Jamie, and everything you've just said confirms that he's a creep. I reckon he's found a way to jump into people's dreams and then mess that person up. He's going to try and kill me tonight."

Jamie shook her head. "Whatever. He wouldn't do that. I know Richard."

"I need you to call it off Jamie. You need to speak to him, and convince him to leave me and Monique alone."

"I can't, Stacey."

"You'd better, or else."

"He isn't at my house Stacey."

"Where is he?"

"He's in a coma. He fell apart, and now he's plugged into a machine at the Catholic nursing home."

Jamie slung her satchel over her shoulder, and snatched the paper list from me. She tied her hair up in a pink scrunchie.

"Stay away from my family," she said. "My brother is sick. He's not a phantom killer. Grow up."

The school bell at the top of the chapel rang to announce the start of the day. Jamie stormed off, leaving me to stash the figurines back into my satchel. I pushed my bag strap over my shoulder, and yawned. Then I yawned again. The bench next to the bubblers looked comfortable.

I lowered my satchel, and was about to curl up there and then, when I saw dad's car. It tore through the parking lot, narrowly avoiding a pedestrian, and mounted the curb. My dad tumbled out of the car, and started running towards the admin building.

"Dad!" I called out.

He stopped, and saw me sitting behind the Arts and Sciences building. He approached me with his `head lowered.

"What is it dad?"

"Hey sweetie," dad said quietly. "Monique's parents just called me."

VIII

There was only one hospital in town, and it was a ten-minute walk from the school. The brain ward's young doctor had an annoying habit of tapping his pen against his teeth. He was keeping time with the beeps of the ECG. He might have been handsome if he'd bothered to moisturise his face more often. I could see Monique's feet sticking out from behind the tan curtain that had been drawn around her cot. The doctor's smile was stained blue as I approached.

"You a relative?" he asked.

Through the gap in the curtain, I could see Monique's mum sitting beside the bed. Before I could answer, I was buried in Mrs Brown's ample bosom.

"Stacey!" Mrs Brown jiggled as she wept. "Monique hasn't woken up."

I pulled myself away from her suffocating hug, and peeked inside. Monique's arms were both in slings. It resembled a straight-jacket. Her nose was full of tubing. A half-full catheter bag was strapped to the leg of the bed. Normally Monique had beautiful curly locks, but they were now plastered to her face with a fevered sweat.

"What happened to her arms?" I asked.

"We don't know the exact cause," the doctor said, taking a corner of the mattress to consult her chart. "The ultrasound revealed that there's a lot of ligament damage."

"Did something happen at school yesterday?" Mrs Brown asked me, patting Monique on the head.

The doctor shook his head. "This wasn't a small sports injury. She has a forced torsion of both her humeri, leading to both her shoulders dislocating. Has some deep rib bruising too. She would have gone home screaming from the pain."

Mrs Brown looked at the doctor with renewed horror. "You don't think someone did this to her during the night, do you?"

"Right now, the fact that she hasn't woken up is far more concerning than her dislocated arms. We've seen a few other cases of it this year. Kids going to bed and never waking up again."

Mrs Brown's hand went to her mouth, and my hand curled to a fist.

"Oops, sorry. Monique seems like a strong girl though," the doctor quickly added. "She'll recover soon, I'm certain."

The doctor stood and excused himself, and drew the curtain behind him as he left. Mrs Brown continued to hold me close for comfort

"The doctor told me it's very possible she can hear us," Mrs Brown said. "Is there anything you want to say to Monique, Stacey?"

I kissed Monique on her sweaty forehead. Then I leaned in close to whisper in her ear.

"I'm going to go and pay Richard a little visit."

IX

"I haven't seen you here before," the nursing-home receptionist said through a cigarette. "Who are you seeing?"

"They let you smoke here?" I asked.

She took a big drag, and exhaled directly in my face. "Sure, as long as I don't do it when the sensitive guests arrive in the afternoon. Why do you think the whole place smells like pine air freshener?"

I wrote *Jamie Smith* on the sign-in book. The nurse spun the guest register around and looked at the name carefully, and then at me. I held her gaze evenly.

Richard was in a room with one other coma patient. I closed the door. He'd lost weight. His acne had cleared up, and his hair had grown longer. Richard now resembled a blonde-haired rock star, and actually looked pretty cute.

My head dropped to my chin from exhaustion, and I heard Monique screaming.

I jolted back to the nursing home. Richard's saline bag was nearly empty. His heart rate was being monitored by an ancient ECG that beeped and buzzed. A metal crash cart was parked in the corner of the room, which was probably against regulation.

I lifted up the dust blanket on the crash cart, and looked underneath. There was a row of packaged syringes, fresh saline bags, and little else. I took one of the empty syringes, and ripped it from its plastic. Trembling, I held it for a long time, looking at Richard as he lay there. A little air in the vein, and Richard would be dead.

"Sorry about this," I said. "But I really need to sleep."

I held the syringe with shaking fingers, and drew air into its chamber. I popped the drip out of Richard's wrist, and aimed the tip of the syringe into his cannula. I hesitated. Could I really kill such a good-looking guy? I withdrew the syringe, and dropped it.

In the recesses of my mind, something was troubling me about the whole situation. If I killed Richard, would it really free Monique from her coma, or would she be trapped forever? I thought back to Monique's name written on Richard's hit list, in all capitals, beside Derek's name. Was it a coincidence?

The door closed behind me as I left the room. Richard slept peacefully.

X

Despite my urgent need for sleep, I found it difficult to get comfortable in bed. The small unicorn night light had been replaced, at my request, with a simple amber lamp that plugged into the wall socket. Dad had suggested I wear my waterproof undies tonight—in case I had more night terrors. I'd protested, but then agreed to it. I shifted around in bed, trying to get comfortable. My undies made crackling sounds when I moved.

It was the first night in years since Monique and I didn't talk on the phone. I tried to call Derek and talk, but he said he was too busy to talk tonight. I pulled the photo of Monique, Derek, and I down from my bedside table, and held it aloft to look at it. Monique looked stunning in a blue tutu she'd managed to procure for the sports carnival. She'd also found some matching fairy wings from the cheap shop. I'd painted her face in blue warpaint: Aztec patterns. Monique had won best-dressed.

Derek was there in casual clothes, running to catch up with us as the picture was taken. His arm stretched out towards my waist.

I looked again. His elbow was straight. I tilted my head.

Monique was looking at the camera, wide-eyed, with her pelvis pushed forward. Derek's arm, Monique's surprise, Derek's eyeline. Derek wasn't looking at me. He was reaching out towards Monique. Then it crystallised in my mind: why was Monique surprised by the camera? Because in the photo, Derek was pinching Monique's butt.

I threw the picture frame at the wall. It dented the plasterboard, and landed face-down on the carpet. I heard the protective glass break, and then sobbed into my pillow.

XI

I was seated in the audience, looking up at the stage. The crowd buzzed with excitement as the curtain lifted.

"What's the production?" I asked the nursing mother who was seated next to me.

"This one is called *The Torture of Monique*," the lady said. "It's a classic."

She returned to cooing at the young child in her arms. I recognised her voice, and the shape of her mouth while she spoke.

"Mum?" I asked.

She turned to me, and I realised she was me. This version of me was much older, and looked upsettingly similar to my mother. I recognised the baby from my childhood photo albums.

"Pardon me."

"Could you keep it down?" said a deeper voice from behind. This version of myself was bald, and wore a University of Queensland cap to cover it.

"Sorry."

The lights switched on, and Derek stepped out onto the stage.

He was pushing a table on wheels in front of him, with a blanket draped over it. Two lumps stuck out either side of the table, concealed by the blanket. Derek carefully parked the table at centre-stage. The audience and I leaned forward in anticipation.

As I watched, Derek flickered between a younger version of myself, then my mother with the wide grin, and then back to Derek again. He was all of my nightmares, coalesced into one person.

"Stacey." Derek let the word ring out into the air confidently. "I'm glad you've returned. I think Monique is ready to tell you the truth now."

"Why don't you tell me the truth first, Richard?" I yelled out.

"Shh," hissed the bald version of me.

"Shut up." I stood up on my seat. "Go on Richard, I know that's you inside Derek."

My boyfriend paused, with his next line caught in his throat. Even from this distance, I could see him swallow the lines he had prepared to say next.

"Are you sure that's what you want?" he asked. "I thought you'd prefer this version..."

"Hurry up," I called out. I planted my foot firmly on the chair in front of me. "Stop wasting my time."

I could see the gears turning in Derek's mind, which was a dead-giveaway that it wasn't Derek standing there. Then he shrugged.

For a moment, nothing happened. Then, a red spot grew on Derek's face: a pimple. It was the size of a coin, but it swelled to the size of a golf ball, and then a basketball. The crowd, including me, groaned unison. The pimple pushed Derek's facial features aside, towards his neck and ears. A large yellow nub appeared in the middle of the giant pimple, where his nose should have been. Derek's hands reached up and gingerly prodded at the swollen head. He squatted slightly on the stage.

"Don't touch it," the mother beside me called.

"You'll only make it worse," yelled a version of me who looked like a beauty vlogger.

Both of Derek's hands pushed roughly at the tender flesh. The yellow head resisted for a brief moment, before it erupted with pus. The front row was doused in it.

From the pimple slid all manner of atrocities: a black worm of dirt oozed its way out, followed by a lot of blood. Derek kept squeezing. The pus became a torrent of oily sebaceous liquid, mixing with the blood as it gushed through the hole that now had formed in Derek's once-ideal features.

With one last squeeze, something cocooned in pus and blood burst out of the pimple, ripping the skin to tatters. The cocoon stood triumphantly, fists in the air like Rocky. The body of Derek collapsed like the jumping castle dad had rented for my fifteenth birthday.

"Richard?" I asked.

The cocoon wiped away at the globs of oil and blood stuck to his face. It was Richard, or at least it vaguely resembled him. The boy on stage was much uglier than Richard had ever been. His facial features were distorted and unsymmetrical. As he stood there, I could see the acne throb across his face. It would appear in patches across the corners of his mouth, and then fade away to pink scars, only to suddenly be replaced with a new crop of zits along his neck and forehead. These too faded. Constellations of bright red spots were born and then died in a matter of moments as he stood there.

"Here I am," Richard said proudly, scooping globs of oil from his body and hurling it into the audience, much to our dismay. "Did you miss me Stacey? I've sure missed you."

"What's this all about Richard?" I shouted at the stage.

I could see him peering against the floodlights above, trying to spot me in the crowd. I must have been obscured by the glare because he gave up, and began talking to the audience as a collective again.

"It's about love, Stacey." He stopped, and picked at his face idly. "No wait, it's the other thing. It's about revenge, Stacey."

"I'm sorry I hurt you," I yelled. "I know you're mad at Monique and me. In fact, I'm not too fond of Monique right now either. However, I think we should reason this out. No more weird visits in my dreams."

"Not quite sure what you mean there," Richard said. He cocked his head to one side. "I was irreparably hurt by you, yes, but I don't blame you for that."

"Oh," I said. I pulled my foot back and got off my chair. "Then why are you tormenting me in my dreams?"

"I wasn't after you," Richard called back with a raised eyebrow.

He pulled the blanket off the table, revealing Monique laying down in a magician's box, trapped. Her feet kicked, as she tried to put her knee through the roof of her wooden prison. Her head looked around, and spotted the audience of me watching. Monique looked bad. Her hair was matted, and her face was covered in sweat.

"Stacey!" she begged. "Stacey help me."

Richard wrapped the blanket around his shoulders as a cape, and then pulled a coping saw out the folds in the garment. "I've always been a bit of a magic fan, both real and pretend. My lovely assistant and I have been hard at work, preparing each of these delectable treats for you tonight."

He turned to Monique, brandishing the saw blade. Her eyes were saucers as the sawblade sliced through the air.

"Now, let's do it just like we did in rehearsal," Richard said in a loud stage-whisper. He gave a wink to the audience. Stepping around behind the box, he held the saw aloft and began the interrogation. "Tell us all how you feel about Derek."

I was frozen in place by the spectacle of it all. Richard was confident, in a way I'd never seen before. Every word was carefully enunciated. Every action was bold and meticulously practised.

Monique bit her lip, and scanned the audience for a friendly face. She took in a deep breath.

"I've always liked Derek," Monique began. A gasp went out from the audience.

"Since when?" the bald me heckled.

"Since you started liking him. I never really cared about anyone, except you of course Stacey." She blew a strand of hair off her face. "The way you talked about Derek, the way you idolised him, it really got in my head, you know. I started noticing the same things you did. I started feeling the way you did."

Richard threw his arms wide, and the audience applauded politely.

"Now folks, that first trick was just a little sampler. However, I'm sure the savvier audience members caught the trick. Did you notice it Stacey?"

I nodded, even though he couldn't see it.

He grinned wide. "Monique just lied to you."

He brought the blade down towards the box and began to saw into it. Monique screamed, feet kicking. I scooted past the young mother with an apology. Other versions of myself lifted their legs or pivoted out of the way. I scrambled past another ten versions of myself and made it to the aisle. Richard saw me step out, and stopped sawing. He held the blade aloft again, dripping with blood.

"In the second part of this trick, Monique will outline the exact nature of her relationship with Derek."

Monique's face was pale and gaunt. She sucked in air through clenched teeth.

"We were seeing each other," she said at last. "I met up with him in secret when you liked him, and even a few times after you started dating."

I was expecting the admission, but it still felt like Monique had stabbed me.

"You saw Derek at the school play?" I asked.

Monique nodded with difficulty. Her eyes lowered so that she couldn't see the shaking heads of the audience members.

"Why Monique? You knew I wanted to confess how I felt after the play."

Monique laughed, but it wasn't a nice laugh. "That's exactly why I did it, Stacey. I was angry at you. I've hated you for a long, long time."

I staggered, and the movement caught her eyes. She twisted

around to see me better.

"You must have known it, surely?"

I shook my head, aghast.

Monique rolled her eyes. I'd seen her do the gesture a thousand times, but it was always at someone else's expense.

"Think about it, Stacey. Before you came to school, I was the undisputed queen. I was worshipped by everyone: teachers and students alike. That all changed when you arrived in middle school. You were beautiful. Word got around with the teachers that you'd had a traumatic death in the family, and that there was a divorce coming up. They doted on you. Gave you the best seats in class, looked the other way when you submitted work late, let you sign up to a whole slew of opportunities. They even offered you middle school captain. You stumbled into the school and dethroned me in a matter of weeks, without even trying. I had to befriend you."

I approached the stage, walking slowly so that I didn't spook Richard.

"I didn't know that," I said. "You never told me."

"Of course, I didn't tell you!" she yelled, letting her head flop backwards in exhaustion. "I knew it wasn't going to take long before you realised how much attention you were getting. That's why I called you every night. That's why I taught you how to sway your hips and apply lip gloss. If *I* wasn't going to be the sole object of affection anymore, at least I could team up with you and recover a little of the glory."

I arrived at the stage, and rested my elbows on the wooden floorboards. Richard had his eyes closed, making the sharp movements of a conductor.

"You saw me as a threat? That's stupid Monique, you're

far more beautiful than me."

Monique gave me a withering look.

"Don't you dare," she said at last. "Your low self-esteem is what I hate the most about you Stacey. Either you're the naivest person I've ever met, or you're fishing for compliments at my expense. Quite frankly, I can't decide which of those two things revolts me more."

"Boys think you're pretty as well," I said quietly.

Monique scoffed at that as she looked up at the ceiling. "Oh yeah, great. Eight boys publicly confessed their love for you last term. One boy wrote a poem about your eyebrows. I'm lucky to get a second glance next to you."

"Most boys are just scared of you Monique."

"And they should be scared." She bared her teeth. "They should come crawling to me, begging for a date. They should scurry away when I turn them down." Monique blew a strand of hair out of her eyes. "We're the same, you and me. Our hearts were cut from the same rock."

"Did you catch that?" Richard asked.

I pulled myself up on the stage, and stood over Monique.

"You're lying again," I said. "I can tell."

Richard began sawing again, and Monique screamed.

"Stop!" I shouted, but Richard kept sawing. I grabbed at the blade, but it continued to cut into the wooden box with the incredible strength Richard possessed in this dream. He continued to cut into the box until he reached the midpoint, and then paused.

"Tell Stacey what you told me, Monique," Richard said. He reached down and squeezed the sweat from her hair like it was a sponge.

"Derek said he wanted someone shy and feminine, so I taught you how to be more confident. I taught you the thrill of having the whole school looking at you as you tore someone down. I told you that you should destroy your current boyfriend in front of Derek, so he knows you're available, because I thought it'd be a good way to make him forget about you. Turns out Derek is an airhead, and he doesn't really care what's on the inside. So, he started dating you, and I took what I could on the side."

I bent down and cradled her head in my hands. "You miscalculated on that one."

"Tell her about me," Richard said.

"I got you to date unpopular boys who could give us shopping money. I wanted new things, and I knew you'd take the blame for being fickle." She sniffed loudly. "Except that's not how life works. The other boys just liked you even more, because they thought, *when I get my chance, I won't fail like Richard did.*"

I let go of her head gently, and faced Richard across the box that was bleeding.

"Richard," I began. "How come we keep meeting in our dreams, even after we stopped using the idols?"

Richard smiled. "Those figurines connect your subconscious to mine. You can stop using them, but everyone who sleeps on them will return here to my dream, forever."

"I'll always come here each night?" I asked.

"That's right. Sorry." He shrugged apologetically. "You weren't meant to get caught up in this. Don't get me wrong though, I'm thrilled. All these years, I knew that you really did love me. The only reason you broke up with me was because

Monique and Derek corrupted you."

I smiled warmly at Richard. He was wrong, of course. I broke up with him because back then I didn't like him, but he didn't need to know that. Besides, things were different now: Richard had gotten hot.

I leaned against the box seductively. "Richard, I want to give you a part-time job."

Richard rocked backwards in surprise. "Wow, are you sure about that? In this economic climate?"

I nodded. "I'm certain. Here's how it's going to work, Richard: I'm going to be your girlfriend."

"What?" Monique and the audience shouted in unison.

I addressed the audience, putting my hands up to placate them. "Just hear me out everyone. Right now, I have a 'best friend' who has been scheming behind my back for most of my delicate adolescent life. I also now have access to a nice, loyal boy who I dated in the past, who can control dreams, instead of letting me face the nightmares that I used to."

Richard's mouth was agape. He squirmed a little and blushed. "Well, I mean. I could certainly build some nice dreams, so you can rest."

I blew Richard a kiss.

XII

Recently, my life has been a lot better. If anyone passed by *Our Lady of Knock High School* on Sunday, around lunchtime, they would have noticed a procession of students and teachers arriving for Monique's memorial service. She had died after several days of fevered dreaming, and Richard had let me watch while he broke her each night.

I demanded to lead the service, of course. Monique had been my closest friend. I also gave a very touching speech about what she meant to me as a person. In fact, I read Richard's spell to describe our friendship. I altered it of course, so that it made more sense:

May Monique and I cleave.
May our love for each other be fixed,
With happiness garnished.
May we wear and weather true friendship.

I now believe in Richard's spells. It'd be impossible not to, considering how effective the statuettes were. The spell he had written on the statuettes had come true as well.

I approached Derek after the service.

"Derek," I said. I threw my arms around him, but he was distant. His eyes were glassy as he looked at the large, framed picture of Monique on the assembly stage. "Are you okay?"

"Yeah, I'm fine." Derek said. He wiped at his eyes. "Can I talk to you later Stacey? I kind of need to be alone right now."

"Of course." I reached into the cute purse I'd bought for the memorial service, and I pulled out a white statuette that resembled a man being drawn and quartered. "I know this is strange," I said. "But I think Monique would have wanted you to have this. You're supposed to sleep with it under your pillow, it's like a dreamcatcher."

Derek nodded, and took the sleep idol. "I'll see you around Stacey," he said.

"Promise me you'll put it under your pillow," I said, touching his arm. "It was important to her."

"Yeah, sure." Derek pulled away, muscles rippling.

I allowed myself a faint smile.

"My boyfriend can mess you up," I whispered under my breath.

Students were milling around the auditorium, and slowly gravitating towards the refreshments that the school had put out. I applied a new coat of lip gloss, courtesy of my new best friend.

"I'm so sorry about Monique." Jamie said. She was practically glowing in her long black dress that she wore for the occasion. "Are you sure you're going to be okay? I thought you said those idols were bad news."

"I made a terrible mistake," I lied. I took her hands into my own. "I'm alive and well, as you can see. There was nothing magical about those statuettes. It was all in my head."

Jamie nodded with relief. "Thank goodness. I was scared that I was hurting people with them, but that's silly isn't it? It was all just a strange set of circumstances."

I squeezed her closely. "There's nothing to be afraid of. Not anymore."

In the crowd, I spotted a junior who had taken unsolicited photos of me playing volleyball last week, despite me telling him to stop.

"Jamie, I'll talk to you on Monday."

I checked over my shoulder to make sure Jamie was distracted. Then I approached the junior with a warm smile painted across my face, and the other statuette clasped in my hands.

This figurine had its eyes gouged out.

Finale

I sat up in bed screaming, and felt the familiar dampness across my body. I'd sweat through my pyjamas again. A heavy thumping sound approached, and then my bedroom light switched on. Kalauni stood in the doorway, with her hand still resting on the floor lamp's switch. Her dress was thin, floral, and bright blue, reaching to the floor. Kalauni had slept with her hair unfastened, and it was now a shock of tightly-curled locks that stuck out from her head in every direction.

"The wolf again, Paige?" she asked in her thick, Tongan accent.

Kalauni entered my bedroom without waiting for the reply, and her physical presence alone dispelled any lingering fear. She sat on the corner of the mattress, and I scooted over. Kalauni placed an enormous hand atop my head and prayed under her breath.

"I saw the wolf eat Grandma, over and over."

The middle-aged woman raised her eyebrows: an invitation for me to continue.

"What happened to Grandma's spirit? Where is she?"

Kalauni lifted her hand and watched me for a long time through her brown eyes. "Your Grandma was a good lady. She gave you her weapon, and you killed the wolf. Don't worry about the things outside of your control."

"What if she didn't move on well?" I asked. "What if she's still trapped somewhere?"

Kalauni patted my hip through the fabric of my blanket. "I've asked for help, and we'll receive it. Don't worry about your Grandma until we have news of her spirit's whereabouts."

I nodded, but I knew the dreams would return again tomorrow. For my entire life, it had been Grandma, her lessons, and me. Now it was just me, and what I could remember from her lessons.

Kalauni could read me easily. "You want breakfast early, boss?"

I'd been living with Kalauni for three months now. She'd said it was until I could 'find my feet', and I had nodded like I understood what that meant.

Kalauni lived on the mountain. Her place was a modernist house from the '70s, constructed as a patchwork of roughly poured concrete, darkly-oiled timber, and glass. Kalauni would often stare out at the subtropical forest that grew around us. She often sighed, and told me that she missed the smell of the ocean. Her sons were both adults and lived somewhere far away. Her husband had died, but she wouldn't talk about it.

I'd arrived on her doorstep, after stalling the Mitsubishi all the way up to the small town of Montville, where Kalauni painted landscapes, and threw pottery for a living.

She'd smiled at me warmly when I'd arrived with my suitcase at her workshop, unannounced. Before I had said anything, Kalauni had read my face, held out her arms, and said, "I always wanted a girl."

So that was Kalauni, who was always moving about when others sat. Who somehow always had food in the oven, and never burned it. Who smelled like meat cooked beneath the earth. She was a barely-controlled whirlwind, just like her hair.

When Kalauni brought me upstairs to eat at four o'clock in the morning, Matilda was already at the dining table, dabbing her mouth with a serviette. Matilda was the other artist-in-residence, who lived in the downstairs portion of the house.

The downstairs area was in a constant state of mess: stacked high with books, newspapers, and sketches of fat women that she never let me look at. Matilda was perhaps the necessary counter-force in Kalauni's life. She was a forty-something Japanese woman, cold and thin. A lover of poetry and architecture, and little else.

"How's the writing?" I asked. Matilda had brought up some light reading, so I slipped into a chair that wasn't stacked high with books.

"It's terrible," Matilda said. It was impossible to tell

whether she was writing an architecture article, or a love poem, because she wore the same frustrated expression for both as she typed onto an antique electric-typewriter that supposedly helped her write better. Generally, she would wring her hands for days on end and make no progress, and then one morning Matilda would have written half a book.

Kalauni placed a plate of scrambled eggs on toast in front of me, the first plate of many, and began neatly stacking the piles of discarded books that lay across the table. The last guest to breakfast was perhaps the oddest. He was a spirit about the height of a piano stool, and his body had the proportions of a teddy bear. He couldn't recall his name from before he died, and he now dozed a lot, so we called him Noddy.

Noddy climbed atop the electric typewriter, and scratched his perfectly-round head while he watched me eat. Matilda typed a few words through his torso, and then threw up her hands and picked up the newspaper instead.

"Why do you bother reading that thing?" Noddy asked, in his quiet voice that sounded like wind chimes. "You could just ask me what's been happening around the world."

Matilda kept the newspaper held between herself and him. "I happen to like the way the editor writes. Lots of flourish, compared to your robotic telegrams."

"What's a telegram?" I asked.

"Not now Paige. Kalauni, can you come and take this thing away from me, please?"

Kalauni swept Noddy up in her arms, and tickled his belly. "Don't worry yourself about her. I happen to like hearing your reports."

Noddy squirmed in her arms, until she deposited him atop

of the stove. Noddy raised his pudgy arms above his head to form a perfect circle, and then began to sing out his report. "Accessing Gaia. Guardian agency in Melbourne sends regards. Ask if you need any assistance caring for Gretel's girl."

My ears perked up at the mention of my Grandma's name.

Kalauni looked over her shoulder at me. "Ahem, let's come back to that one later."

Noddy did a pirouette on the hot stove, unaffected by the heat. "The Brisbane agency would like assistance tracking siren near the Sunshine Coast."

"What's a siren?" I asked.

"It's a twisted soul who attacks young men," Matilda said, without looking up from her newspaper.

"Paige, why don't you go play?" Kalauni used the tone of voice that told me it wasn't a suggestion. "I've got to send a message to Brisbane."

I deposited my dirty plate in the sink, and went to collect my balestra.

* * *

In the backyard, I had arranged a makeshift training course for myself. I fastened the balestra across two clips on my belt. Then I strapped my axe to my right thigh, with its blade sheathed in a leather strap.

I always began my training routine with the ten-metre knotted rope, which was fastened to the lowest limb of a red cedar. I climbed hand over hand, my feet meeting together so I could find a grip against the knots of rope. By the time I reached the tree limb, my arms were burning, and I had to huff in the icy mountain air with great empty breaths.

I love you Grandma, but why did you give me such bulky

195

weapons?

I perched atop the tree limb. The wind was blowing through the tree canopy, biting at my fingers and nose. I gripped the branch with just my legs, and unclipped the balestra from my waist. The wind blew a sudden gust, and I squeezed my knees together even more tightly. Beneath my hoodie, and over my shirt, I wore a compact quiver designed for holding crossbow bolts. Two weeks ago, I'd cut a hole within the large, central pocket of my hoodie so that I could access the bolts quickly and surreptitiously, if required.

Clinging to the tree branch with my knees, it was impossible to follow proper technique. After training for the past two months on the ground, with the correct stance, I'd realised that one day I'd have to shoot at a target with awkward or uncertain footing.

I pulled the bow back, using my hip as leverage. My already-sore arms screamed in protest. I hated that feeling, because it meant I still wasn't strong enough. Once the balestra was loaded with a bolt, I took aim. A row of Matilda's old beer cans sat on a low, wooden retaining wall in the backward. I felt the wind at my back. I closed my non-dominant eye, and connected the wood of the shaft to my cheek.

Fumpftch. The balestra barely made a sound as it launched the bolt. The clang of the beer can was explosive by comparison. I pulled the string back again, and again, firing shots at the cans until the string slipped from my fingers with exhaustion. Then, I climbed back down the rope again, my hands red and shaking. When I got to the bottom of the rope, I collapsed onto the ground.

Noddy was sitting on a tree stump, watching me. He was

covering his eyes with his hands, but it didn't achieve much, because his hands were translucent.

"I can see you watching me," I said between gasps for air.

"I'm not hiding," he said, but the hands remained in place. "I get nervous when you climb back down. You always have the shakes."

I continued to lie on the cold grass. The sun was beginning to rise up and over the mountain, warming the house. The sky was a pale blue-grey, and covered with wispy clouds as far as the eye could see.

"Am I wasting my time here, Noddy?" I asked. I rubbed my eyes until stars appeared.

"I don't understand. What else would you be doing?"

"Grandma died, and I know the spirit of a guardian is somehow different, but she never climbed out of her grave at sunrise. Is her spirit lost out there, somewhere?"

"I'm afraid Kalauni has forbidden me from telling you anything specific about the guardians," Noddy replied. "Wish I could help."

"She did what?" I sat up. "Why would she do that?"

Noddy opened his mouth, and the voice of Kalauni echoed from his lips. "She needs time to heal, Noddy. Don't go filling her head with information she doesn't need right now."

I felt an angry heat in my chest, choking me as I burst through the kitchen sliding door. Kalauni was cleaning the dishes when I confronted her. I walked around the counter, hands on hips.

"Why won't you talk to me about the guardians?" I asked, letting the ice creep into my voice.

Kalauni sighed and looked up at something inside the

stovetop. Matilda picked up her typewriter and headed for her room downstairs. I continued, unfazed.

"I can make my own decisions." I said, placing the balestra on the kitchen table for emphasis. "I want to become a guardian. I want to protect people like Grandma did, but I don't even know where to start. She sent me to you because she thought you would take over my training."

Kalauni turned to face me with the wooden spoon she'd been using. She wore a sad expression.

"She sent you to me for protection, and I am protecting you, Paige. Being a guardian is not a life you should commit yourself to right now. I allowed you to keep training, begrudgingly, because I thought that having some routine in your life would help you. Understand this, however," she extended her arm, and pointed her wooden spoon at me like it was a sword. "You shouldn't even know about the guardians. I'm baffled about why Gretel trained you at such a young age."

"She wanted me to be like her."

"Most guardians begin training at adulthood. You won't be left behind. There's no magical school where you can make friends and ply the trade of stopping evil spirits. It's just this." Kalauni gestured around the house. "It's normal life, Paige. Guardians go to regular school, they get regular jobs, they get married, and *occasionally* they fight. There's only a select few who can afford to be Batman, and just like Batman, you've got to be independently wealthy."

"So, this is it?" I asked. The small kitchen and homely dining room suddenly seemed suffocating. "You all just sit around and wait for trouble, and then you go back to your lives?"

"We're not the secret service," Kalauni said, rubbing the bridge of her nose. "We're the neighbourhood watch."

"I don't believe that. You and Grandma both have weapons lying about the place. I can tell you've learned magic like she did. You can teach me how to use that, at the very least."

Kalauni shook her head. "The guardians have many powerful abilities, yes. That doesn't mean we're warriors. In an ideal scenario, we don't have to fight. When we fight, some of us die."

"You're not telling me the whole picture."

"Fine." Kalauni spat the word out. "It's not a glamorous existence, Paige. Maybe seeing the spirit world has desensitised you to this simple fact: dying is not pleasant. You forget who you are. You spend a millennium wandering, or you become something else. Something not quite human."

"Like Noddy?"

"Like poor little Noddy."

I kicked a table chair. "So, you won't train me? I just have to go back to school and pretend that none of this world exists?"

Kalauni returned to the stove. "You're just like my husband."

"He died fighting, didn't he?" I asked. "He was a guardian too."

Kalauni kept stirring the pot. "There's a nice high school here, and they'll let you start grade seven next term. When you've graduated, you can decide if you still want to become a guardian."

"That's too long! I can't go to school and be the poor little orphaned girl. You don't get to tell me what to do!" Involuntarily, I stamped my foot, which didn't help my argument.

Kalauni's voice was dark. "I think that's enough, Paige. My boys would have been whipped for talking to me like that."

"I'm glad I'm not your kid then."

I shouldn't have said it. I heard the words leave my mouth as keenly as a crossbow bolt, and they buried themselves inside the softest spot of Kalauni's heart.

"I see."

Her wooden spoon stirred the pot for a moment longer, before she placed it gently back onto the stovetop, and looked up to the heavens. I thought she was going to cry.

"I know you're grieving, and I understand what it means to lose someone." Kalauni spoke in a firm voice that betrayed no emotion. "You may not be my daughter, but I will raise you like my daughter, and I will discipline you the same way. So, listen closely."

"Go ahead."

Kalauni clicked her tongue once, in irritation. It was as loud as a gunshot.

"If you ever speak to me like that again, I will belt you."

I didn't believe her, and I told her so.

She meant it.

* * *

Noddy sat beside me as I rubbed my tender legs and cried. Kalauni was stone-faced, sitting in her small backyard shed. Her bare foot tapped the pedal of her pottery wheel.

"Does it still hurt?" Noddy asked quietly.

"I'm more upset about Grandma," I replied.

Noddy stubbed his toe into his other toe: a gesture of shyness. "Kalauni forbade *me* from telling you anything about the guardians."

"You said that already."

"There is someone who *could* tell you about them," Noddy continued. "If you asked him, then I wouldn't be breaking my promise."

"Who?"

"A great spirit that's been seen in the area. Knows a lot of things. He hitchhiked over here recently, on an airplane from Indonesia."

"Where is he?" I asked.

"Up the mountain, near the shops. He likes watching the fortune tellers and tarot readers."

I stood up, and carefully approached Kalauni as she worked. If she was sorry for belting me, she didn't show it.

"Can I go to the shops?" I asked.

Kalauni smiled. "That sounds like a nice idea. There's five dollars on the kitchen bench if you'd like to buy yourself some candy."

"Thanks."

I turned to leave, but Kalauni stopped me.

"Paige?"

"Yes?"

"No driving. Stretch your legs a bit. You've been working too much on your upper body, and you could hurt yourself."

I went inside with Noddy, and swiped the money off the counter. Outside, I could hear Kalauni complaining. "Fancy teaching a child how to drive. How irresponsible."

"We need to make a phone call," Noddy explained in a

hushed voice, pointing to the yellow pages phone book. "You're looking for someone called Madam Kathy."

I found the business number: a small advertisement next to a cartoon drawing of a crystal ball. I called, and booked an appointment.

* * *

It took me an hour to walk to the fortune teller, who was operating from inside her own house. Outside her suburban home, there was a large sign painted in purples and pinks, proclaiming that these were the chambers of Madam Kathy: open from 9am - 12pm, by appointment.

I knocked, but didn't have to wait long. Kathy came running.

"Come in! Come in!" she said, ushering me inside. Her brown hair was up in curlers, and she was wrapped in a pink silk shawl. "Oh, you didn't come with your parents?"

I ignored the question.

Kathy operated her business out of her living room. The only light came from a salt lamp in the corner. A collection of oddities decorated the room. An enormous dream-catcher hung on the main wall. Strong mint oil burned beneath a tea candle on the coffee table. There was the skull of a dog on the coffee table, which had been skilfully etched and dyed with red and blue spirals.

"Do you like the skull?" asked Kathy, the housewife fortune-teller.

"I haven't seen anything like it before."

"Some believe the pattern has the ability to coax a spirit to remain inside," she explained, tapping the temple of the dog's skull. "This used to be my dog Fido. It's nice knowing that he's inside there, watching me."

I peered inside the eye sockets, and didn't see anything. Then again, an animal's spirit wouldn't manifest itself in the same way a person's spirit would.

We sat cross-legged on her living room's synthetic shag rug, while Kathy read my tea leaves.

"Yes, I hear the spirits saying something," the lady said.

The great spirit Ni sat reclining on a sofa, flanked on either side by two goons. Ni's baby-sized hands covered his enormous mouth as he giggled. Instead of being dressed in shadows like most spirits, his clothing was bound to him with clarity, like flesh. He was fat, fat, fat: rolls of him spilled and billowed out of his ill-fitting suit and cravat. His goons wore matching suits. They looked like mid-level spirits, which meant if they wanted to, they could probably push me over, and try to pin me to the ground.

"You're a kook!" Ni yelled in the lady's ear, as she closed her eyes in concentration. "Tell her this is a sham!"

It took a lot of effort not to look directly at him, as he made faces directly behind Kathy. I pulled my backpack onto my lap.

"What are they saying exactly?" I asked, crossing my arms. I popped my gum loudly.

The lady twitched at the popping noise. "There's someone who wishes to speak to you beyond the veil."

"Who's speaking?" I asked with a sigh. "What's her name?"

"Let me listen. Let me listen," the lady replied. "It's a woman, and she has a message for you."

"Classic," Ni said, shaking his head. "Common girlie, you just gave away that it's a woman who died."

"She says to keep living your life," the medium said to the

young girl. "To remember her fondly, but to let her go now."

"Who's the girl searching for?" one of the goons asked Ni.

"I heard about this one." Ni replied. "It was her Grandma. A guardian. If you can believe that."

"I heard they're nearly extinct," the other spirit goon said.

"Well, this guardian was raising her granddaughter on a farm up North. Was going to teach her the trade or something. Died last year."

"Oh, oh!" I exclaimed. "I can hear the spirits speaking to me!"

"You can?" the entire room asked in unison, including the part-time medium.

"If it's all the same with you," I said, producing a small vial from my hoodie, "I think I'd like to burn my own fragrance."

"Well, I've never had someone request that before," the medium replied, looking about the room in a fluster. "I don't know if it'd be appropriate to..."

I'd already tipped the contents of the vial into the oil burner, however. I sat, staring at the medium.

"What do you think the spirits are saying to you?" the lady asked.

"It's probably not worth repeating," I replied. I locked eyes with Ni, who shifted in his chair.

"Is she looking at you, boss?" one of the goons replied.

I pulled a gas mask from my backpack, and fastened it across my face.

Kathy managed to withstand the drug I was burning long enough to get to her feet, but then she went down to her knees. I caught her head before she hit the coffee table.

"I don't like this," Ni said, standing up. "Did the hag leave the back door open?"

One of the goons ran to the back of the house, and then returned with a frightened expression.

"It's shut. She must've closed it when the girl arrived."

Ni heaved himself to his feet. "Check the windows upstairs. Maybe there's a way out of here."

I stood up and waved at Ni. Judging from the expression on his face, it was the most disconcerting thing he'd seen.

"Do you always watch this medium while she works?" I asked. I squatted next to my open backpack, and examined the assembled group of three spirits around me.

"Sometimes," Ni said. "But I don't like my parties being interrupted. Boys? Grab the creepy girl."

Ni's goons leapt forwards to grab me, but failed to notice that I was pulling something from my bag.

I withdrew the balestra. The first bolt sang through the air, and hit one goon in the left shoulder. The force of the impact carried him through the air, and pinned him to the living room wall. He stared at the bolt, disbelieving.

The other goon lunged forward, and was on top of me. I rolled to the left, and out towards the kitchen, scrambling to fit another bolt into the balestra as I got to my feet and ran.

"Quick!" Ni screamed as he waddled to hide himself behind a sofa. "Get her before she has a chance to reload!"

The second goon came in low at me, and successfully grabed my hood with his fist. He looked back at Ni and grinned widely, "I caught her!"

I cocked a second bolt against the string, and loaded it. The goon turned back around to look down the business end of the balestra as it fired. The bolt was delivered swiftly between his eyes, throwing him back onto the floorboards.

"Ow," he said as he hit the floor.

"It hurts, doesn't it?" said the goon who was stuck to the wall.

I forced myself to take long, controlled breaths through my nose as I gathered myself. I cocked a third non-lethal bolt into the balestra, and entered the living room in a crouch, but there wasn't any need to worry.

"What do you want?" Ni asked in a muffled voice. The great spirit had curled up into a perfect sphere. "I barely rank as a great spirit, there can't be a bounty on my head."

"There's no bounty for you," I agreed, and then levelled my weapon at him. "I hear you can give a girl information if she's persuasive."

"Certainly, certainly!" Ni uncurled, and pulled a wide smile that caused his neck to wobble. "What can I help you with, miss?"

"I need to know where the up-and-coming guardians train. I need to speak with them."

"Oh, that." Ni pulled himself to his feet gingerly, arms struggling to rise above his head in surrender. He plunged himself down on a sofa, but kept his hands raised. "No one knows exactly where they meet. That'd kind of defeat the purpose, wouldn't it? If the spirits found out, the guardians would just shift to a new place."

"But I'm guessing there *are* rumours."

"There are rumours."

"I can work with rumours," I said, and lowered the balestra.

Ni also lowered his hands. "This particular rumour is quite

dangerous. If I told you, and the guardians somehow traced the leak back to me, it would put my afterlife at risk."

"What do you want in return?"

Ni rubbed his tiny hands together in excitement. "A breather who can run errands! The possibilities! I could get you to chase up some favours that the Great Sun Bear Spirit owes me. There's also a leviathan who I want to contact."

I frowned. "Just one possibility please, and you'd better decide on it quickly."

Ni scratched his enormous head.

"A siren's taken up residence near the freeway. She's a nasty piece of work, causing a lot of anxiety for some of my clients that live nearby. If I send you as my personal champion to deal with her..."

"...then you'll earn more notoriety," I concluded. "It's all favours, contracts and politics with you, isn't it?"

Ni shrugged. "What else is there in the spiritual realm? I don't find the other methods of obtaining power particularly appetising."

"Tell me about this siren."

"I want her dead, and then evicted, in that order."

"Why? I can't imagine ordering a hit on a spirit, just because they're strange."

Ni smiled. "She's also sitting on good real estate."

Kathy was still snoring on the floor. I pulled one bolt out of the plasterboard. The goon that had been suspended against the wall fell down to the ground. I pulled the other bolt out of the floorboards. That goon sat up, and began furiously massaging the hole that had been drilled between his eyes.

"Do you want the address?" Ni asked. "It's not too far

from here."

I took out my notepad.

* * *

Noddy and I waited until midnight, when Kalauni's thunderous snores shook the house. Then, I helped Noddy into the Mitsubishi's passenger seat, and we drove for the highway. I sat on the phone book, so I could see over the steering wheel. As a joke, I'd strapped a seatbelt through Noddy's middle.

"Is it legal for you to drive?" Noddy asked curiously, as I swung around a corner.

"Not at all," I said, narrowly avoiding the curb as we swung off the forested highway. "Grandma put a fair amount of magic on the car, so that people feel uncomfortable about looking through the windows."

"I see." We pulled up at a traffic light beside an old man.

"Oi!" I rolled down my window and tried to get the old man's attention. "Look at me, old-timer!"

The gentleman looked dead ahead, obviously trying to avoid eye contact. I rolled the window back up again.

"What do people see when they look at this car?"

"Most folks see a builder in a Holden Ute."

Noddy smiled. "That'd do it."

"Yeah, works like a charm." The lights went green, and we were off again. "Give me the run-down on this siren. What's her pattern of behaviour? Known victims? That sort of thing."

Noddy scratched at his chin.

"First, she preys exclusively on men," he said, counting the facts off on his fingers. "Second, she has a real penchant for body parts. Collects different pieces from the guys she kills.

Oh, and did I mention they were young men? Usually young men. Doesn't have an appetite for older guys."

"Grandma said young souls have more potential energy," I said. "That adds up. So, she's a siren preying on men. That's not particularly unusual. Ni mentioned she made other spirits uncomfortable?"

"Word is that she's trying to take a shortcut towards becoming a great spirit."

"She's not cutting ties to her past life?"

Noddy shook his head. "That's the normal way of doing it. Ni found a shortcut, but he doesn't remember how. He's the new kid on the block as a result. That's why he's got to earn respect through other means. There's probably a whole host of ways to elevate yourself quickly."

"Do you think Ni believes this siren has found a way to fast-track her ascension, and wants her killed before she completes it?"

"Perhaps. Whatever she's doing, she's painted a big target on herself. The guardians and great spirits are talking about teaming up to find her and take her down. Strange times, and stranger bedfellows."

"If the guardians are after her, why send us to do the job first?"

"Ni wants the glory for himself. Can you imagine if the guardians owed him some favours?

There was a procession of spirits walking beside the road tonight: spirits who had a destination, but had to make do with a long trek.

Noddy waved at them. "It's fun to ride inside cars."

"I guess you can't possess a car, can you?" I asked, peering ahead through the headlights.

Noddy laughed. "Maybe Ni could. I heard he went on joyrides when he'd become a newly-awakened spirit. As for me, I'd struggle to possess a pencil."

"What about people?" I asked. "I hear some people are easier than objects to take over. Yoga instructors, for example."

Noddy shook his head, and looked down at his translucent hands. "I've managed to possess a finger. Maybe a hand if the person was distracted. People usually think it's pins and needles, and then shake it off."

As we drove, we passed what looked like shadowy stones scattered along the roadside: spirits who had given up on a destination or a task. They were curled up and perfectly still, waiting for an end that would never come. The sight of them made Noddy particularly uncomfortable.

"The soul needs tasks to complete," he shook his head. "Look at that. They'd probably let you sit on them." He glanced down at the map he was sitting on. "Oh, it's right-hand turn up ahead."

I saw the small, unmarked driveway. It was overgrown with long grass. The branches from overhead trees hung low over the small opening.

"I can see why Ni would like this spot," Noddy said. "It looks just like a spirit portal."

I hit the indicator, and we cruised under the dark foliage. Dirt and gravel crunched under the tyres. I dodged a sinkhole. The driveway dropped away sharply, and I had to creep forward with my foot pounding rhythmically on the brake pedal. I saw that the road ahead now meandered between the trees.

"It's so isolated," I said.

"That's precisely why it's valuable," Noddy said, checking the side-mirror. "Ni's a bit peculiar, in that he likes spending time looking at breathers. Most great spirits want to be left alone by humans. Who wants breathers wandering through them, or building cities and making a racket? So, ghost towns get set up anywhere that's abandoned. You should see Chernobyl at this time of year, it's packed with spirits. Practically a holiday destination. Then there's all those spirits that just go and live at the bottom of the ocean, for the same reason."

I carefully swung around a tall tree with blackened bark. "So, Ni connects powerful spirits with nice spots to live in?"

"Sure, I mean, otherwise it'd be a free-for-all. Ni also offers 'protection' as part of the package, which he outsources to poor fools like you."

"Ni cleans up the neighbourhood for the powerful dead, and in return he gets...what exactly?"

Noddy smiled warmly. "More rumours. More favours. More spirits willing to help him get ahead. It seems to work for him, probably because—"

Noddy stopped. He peered out into the dark tree line.

"What is it?"

"I saw something move out there."

I yanked on the handbrake, causing the car to lurch back and forth with the momentum of stopping abruptly. My crossbow was suddenly on my lap. I must have grabbed it instinctively. I pulled the drawstring back into place and unfastened Noddy's seatbelt, then I pulled my axe from the glove compartment, and fastened it to the studs on my belt.

"You aren't going out there, are you?"

I kicked the car door open, and stepped out onto the gravel road.

"Do you reckon it's the siren?" I asked. "Was there a glow?"

"I couldn't see a glow," Noddy whispered. He clambered over the handbrake towards me.

Leaves crunched underfoot somewhere ahead. They grew quieter and quieter, moving away from us.

"Well, I'm pretty content to sit this one out," Noddy said, crawling into the space between the steering wheel and the pedals.

"If she finds you alone out here," I replied, "I won't be held responsible for you being consumed, or whatever it is she's doing."

Noddy weighed up his options for a moment, and then tumbled out of the car.

"Where do you think she's camping out?" I asked.

"The track keeps going this way." Noddy said, pointing ahead.

We left the car, and made our way forward on foot. No sense driving up with a loud engine, and letting the siren know exactly where we are.

A beautiful singing voice wafted through the air.

"Should we cover our ears?" I asked, checking my crossbow.

Noddy shrugged. "I thought those stories about siren songs were just myths."

"Maybe you're right. Grandma said that men tend to seduce themselves, siren or no siren."

I could just make out the house in the darkness. It was an

antiquated, two-storey, lakeside estate that had once been painted a gaudy orange. Tracks had been worn into the earth from several sets of car tires that approached the lake, and then vanished at the lapping edge. Clerestory windows sat high above us, now dirty and broken, but allowing a view of the upstairs porch that overlooked the lake. A creaking sound cut through the dull wash of waves against the shore.

"After you," Noddy said. "I hear she's fast, and strong."

"Thanks." I checked my balestra again, and then caught myself. *Why am I trying to stall?*

We approached the steps of the house, and the singing grew louder. In the distance, I could hear the sounds of an electric generator purring. A damp smell emanated from inside the house. I took the first wooden step up to the front porch, and heard it protest loudly.

Stupid, Grandma taught you how to use stairs correctly.

I withdrew my foot. Noddy stood well back, looking around anxiously.

"If something happens in there," he whispered, "then I'm going to find a nice object to hide inside."

I jumped up the steps, only using my toes to touch the wood. My feet delicately kissed the edges of the steps, as I launched myself up them. I made it onto the front porch of the property, and peered through the door that hung limply from its frame.

Inside, the distant light of the moon poured through all manner of windows, glass doors, or gaps in the roof. It cast long and crisp shadows that criss-crossed the waterlogged floors, carpets, and abandoned furniture.

I pulled on the front door, but it was rusted in place. A

large window to the left had been broken, so I tried that. The gap wasn't big, and shards of glass jutted out from the four corners of the frame. I put the balestra through first, followed by my head and shoulders.

My eyes caught a faint movement on the second-storey balcony, which overlooked the entire living area of the cottage: a thin ribbon of red linen was blowing in the wind. It had been torn from a larger garment, and had caught on a stray nail that jutted out from the rotting timbers up there.

I inhaled through my nose deeply, and pushed myself onwards, inching forward. I felt the glass as it delicately scraped across my hair and shoulder. I was through.

Broken glass was strewn across the floor and had been trodden on, creating tiny snowflakes of glass that glinted in the moonlight. Behind me, Noddy followed at a distance. The decrepit stairs didn't make a sound as he climbed them.

The singing continued from the floor above.

I crossed the dining room. The carpet underneath my feet sank under my weight. Black water gushed out of the carpet with each step, and filled the footprints I left behind.

Some unrecognisable piece of wooden furniture sat in the middle of the room, now splintered and mangled. Motes of dust mixed with the spores of fungus in the air. At the end of the dining room, a spiral staircase made of rusting steel led up to the open-plan second floor, and the sounds of singing.

I felt Noddy approach behind me, and held my crossbow back behind me, signalling him to wait. I chanced a quick look up the metal stairs. Nothing.

"Wait for me here," I whispered, turning to make sure Noddy had heard me.

He was gone.

I held my breath and scanned the room. The dark shadows didn't betray his familiar luminescence. Upstairs, the singing continued, in a confident soprano. I grasped the rusted guard-rail of the staircase and climbed quickly, balestra pointed ahead.

At the top of the stairs, I saw why this house was a goldmine for Ni. The second floor looked out across the lake through large windows that had long ago been blown in by the weather. The porch still stood, overlooking the bay, but it sagged somewhat in the middle. Facing the lakeside was a tall rocking chair made of old white oak. It creaked as it tipped back and forth. Through the gaps in the chair's back, I could see a figure reclining.

I circled wide as I crept, trying to keep as much distance as I could between the chair and myself. Stepping out onto the porch through one of the broken windows, I saw a woman's hand grasping the arm of the chair. The hand was as pale as porcelain, with long, pink nails that tapered to a point.

I continued to skirt the edge of the porch, until the arms of the lady were revealed. Thin and dainty, her arms rose up and vanished into the short-length sleeves of a lady who watched me with complete disinterest.

Her legs were crossed, and covered in fashionable jeans that were tattered across the knees. Her hair was long and orange. The wind that kicked up from the lake stirred her hair gently as she rocked. The dark circles beneath her eyes ruined her beauty, however. The siren looked as though she hadn't slept in years.

She stopped singing. "May I help you?"

"I'm here on official business," I said, holding my balestra level at the lady. "For the guardians."

The siren glanced at the balestra, and stifled a yawn. "Who are you, really?"

"I'm a guardian in training."

"You don't bear the mark."

The enormous lake behind me lapped at the house, as it tried to claim the rotting timber.

"I've been asked to evict a siren."

"What a fascinating task to be given," the lady said. She closed her eyes and let her head lull backwards as she rocked. "There's no siren here though, only me."

"Perhaps you're unfamiliar with the word." I kept my eyes locked on the lady, but searched for Noddy in my periphery. "It's a spirit who preys on young men."

At this the lady chuckled, and opened her eyes again. "Bless you. However, I'm not a spirit. Come and feel my skin, and you'll realise I'm very much human."

I shook my head. "If I did that, and you were some sort of powerful spirit, I'd be dead in seconds."

The lady uncrossed her legs and sat up in her seat. "What makes you think you're not already dead?"

I pulled the trigger. A bolt sang through the air, and embedded itself deep in the wood of the rocking chair. The chair flipped backwards with a crash, but the lady was a blur of movement, and was already standing beside me. She placed a cold hand upon my shoulder.

"I liked that chair."

I tried to duck out of the lady's grasp, but her grip was powerful and strong. The long, pink nails dug into my shoulder. I watched, helpless, as she pulled the axe off my belt and tucked it under her arm. Then Grandma's balestra was pried from my numb hand. The siren released my shoulder, and I staggered back to the porch railing, clutching my bloodied shoulder tightly. The initial excitement I had felt turned to ice-cold fear. She was human, and she was fast.

The lady held the balestra carefully, examining it with interest. "I used to be quite fascinated by history," she said. "I even applied to study it at university."

I watched the siren carefully. I could feel the quiver of bolts inside my hoodie pocket press against my skin. *Slow movements. Wait for an opening.*

"But as time went on, I became more interested in the history of magic, spirits, and the like. Things you can't major in, at any university. It's a shame really. Knowing the past is like having a superpower. You have foresight: a clarity of what to do next."

"Why not go and study then? Why kill young men?" I asked. Slowly, I twisted my body away from the siren, and snaked my left hand inside my pocket and the quiver.

"I've only ever killed when necessary," the siren said with a smile. "Now my boyfriend, on the other hand, has a real temper. If someone ever crosses me, I can always trust him to deal with it. He takes people apart from the inside, through their dreams."

"So, this boyfriend of yours, where is he now?"

The siren looked at her watch. "He died a year ago, but as you and I both know, that doesn't count for much in the grand scheme of things. I know about the weakness of the body, and I know about the power of the spirit."

"How?"

She looked up from her watch. "I like your energy. I used to be a bundle of it, you know. My friend and I from high school—and I can't remember her name—would get up to all sorts of harmless fun together."

"So, how were you exposed to the spirit world?"

"I communed with Richard's spirit through dreams for years before he died. I became pretty accustomed to the spiritual world, because of those dreams. How did you begin to see spirits?"

"Through stories my Grandma told me."

She nodded. "Dreams and stories. Now *there's* true power. Still, the body has its uses."

The siren pulled the string of the balestra back, and fired it at me. Luckily, no bolts had been loaded. The balestra's string rang loudly as it fired with no bolt loaded.

"Bang!" she yelled, and then broke into a fit of giggles. "This is pretty fun."

"So, what's the plan?" I asked, trying to stall. "Are you looking for your boyfriend? Are you trying to find his spirit?"

She shook her head. "I know exactly where his spirit is. My father used to tell me a fairy tale, where people who lived near a castle were put inside objects."

"I've heard that one as well."

"I know where his spirit is trapped, but I that isn't worth anything. I want him back here, in the flesh. I want to see him all the time, not just when I have nightmares. Have you ever been in love? No, what am I saying? You're far too young."

"I loved my Grandma."

"Yes, your Grandma again. Is that why you're running

after spirits? To find out where she is?"

I didn't answer, but I didn't have to.

The siren stepped closer to me. "I also want to bring back the person I love, and I know how to do it."

"I see."

"You've felt the sting as well, haven't you? How can you continue living if you know there's a way to see them again? It's the curse of death: not for those that die, but for those of us who have to continue onward."

The lady stepped closer again. She wiped a tear from her bloodshot eyes.

"I've been alone for so long...would you like to see him?" She bent down to look me level in the eyes. Her pupils were struggling to focus.

Deep in my pocket, the fingers of my left hand danced across the shaft of a balestra bolt. I could stab the siren with it: one quick swing at this distance, and I could try to bury the shaft into her neck like a dagger.

I hesitated, and then released my grip on the bolt.

"Okay, miss."

The siren smiled at me. "Call me Stacey."

* * *

Stacey took me downstairs. I scanned the house for any sign of Noddy, but he wasn't anywhere to be seen. First, we went down the metal staircase, and then we descended a few wooden steps set into the rear of the house. A large basement had been carved into the limestone beneath the cottage. Black and white mould grew along the walls, and a door greeted us at the bottom.

"This room used to be a research lab for a marine

biologist," Stacey explained. "Died a long time ago, now."

She pushed lightly on the basement door. Rows of mortise locks that should have secured the door had been pried loose from the frame. Stacey kicked aside a locking mechanism that lay on the floor.

"Sorry about the mess."

She switched on a low ceiling bulb, which hung from the roof by a frayed cord. The room was half-submerged in water.

Along the walls were racks of tools, now brown and rusted. Dusty jars lined the walls, filled with the shapes of fish. One shelf was rotten and had toppled over onto its side. Many of the other shelves looked as though they might also tumble any minute.

Stacey stepped into the murky water that had flooded the room, letting her jeans get soaked up to the middle of her shins. I plunged into the cold water after her, and it reached all the way up to my knees. I saw tiny fish, the size of a toothpick, dart to and fro across my toes.

There's no way I can fight in here.

Stacey placed my balestra and axe high on a shelf, where I'd struggle to reach it.

"Don't go near the broken display cabinet," Stacey said. "There's some shattered glass over there that I keep finding with my feet."

"Why don't you drain the room?" I asked.

"This is just temporary," Stacey said, wading to the centre. The water churned as hidden creatures beneath the surface fled from her wake. "This isn't exactly ideal living quarters, I just needed somewhere secluded, so I can conduct the ritual. Don't want any neighbours coming and asking questions."

In the centre of the room was a steel table, covered by a clean white tablecloth. It was the only thing that looked clean in the entire room. Stacey whipped the tablecloth away, and stashed it on one of the decaying shelves. Atop the table was a freezer, chugging along. Its power cable was duct-taped to the ceiling, attached to an extension cable that sagged down towards the water, before snaking out of a small window. Outside, I could hear the faint hum of a petrol generator.

"Come have a look. I've been dying to show someone."

She yanked the freezer door open so I could see. I dodged something long and serpentine under the water, and peered over the lip of the freezer.

There was a corpse inside, illuminated by the cold light.

It was male, nude, and had been stitched together: a piecemeal assortment from different bodies. The crown of the head had been scalped from a man with long, blonde hair, like a rock star. There weren't any eyes, just the hollow sockets of a skull, with flesh moulded to it.

"No eyes, I'm afraid." Stacey said, stroking the hair of the corpse. "Richard had bright, blue eyes. But I found the right dimensions for everything else."

"Will he be able to talk?" I asked.

"He should be able to, according to the stories."

"What if that part of the story was embellished?"

Stacey smirked. "I doubt it."

Crossing the room, she opened a dirty glass cabinet with books inside. She dug a few out, setting them to one side, and then pulled out a simple hardback, with yellow and brown pages.

"The incantation is very simple," Stacey said.

She closed her eyes, held the book open in front of her, and then sniffed the pages. Nothing happened for a few moments, but then the words and glyphs painted on its pages were sucked into her nostrils. She opened her eyes. They glowed a piercing, radiant blue.

Stacey deposited the book back into the glass cabinet, and withdrew two statuettes made of bone. I recognised the paintwork: the reds and blues painted on them were similar to the dog skull I had seen in Madam Kathy's house.

"Here's the problem I've faced, little one." Stacey's voice sounded ancient. "Richard's soul was trapped inside these two figurines. Turns out, upon death, a spirit can inhabit an object if they have a deep attachment to it. If he'd only made one of them, then I could have simply broken the idol, and voila. In this case, however, he was split. If I cracked them open, there was no guarantee that they'd fuse back together. I'd be left with two spirits, but they wouldn't necessarily be Richard."

"You need a body," I said. "Then you can try and fuse them together."

"That's right. This sort of stuff is tricky to research: the necessary texts were destroyed by the guardians." She gestured to the books in the glass cabinet. "Hence all the dusty books. I've tried to construct the perfect container for Richard. Something that will feel like himself, like he used to be."

"Why do you think the guardians tried to destroy that information?"

Stacey shrugged. "Why does anyone with authority do anything? To keep it."

"I'm not so sure," I replied. "Maybe they had a good reason to be afraid."

I circled around the freezer.

It was clear to me now that Stacey's method of resurrecting her boyfriend would be useless to me. I didn't have a little flask with Grandma's spirit trapped inside. Even if I did, I wasn't going to make a golem and put her body inside.

My other concern was Stacey.

Just because she wants to show me the ceremony, doesn't mean she'll let me leave.

I judged the height of the shelf where my balestra was. If Stacey succeeded in resurrecting her boyfriend, I didn't want things to go all Frankenstein on me. It'd be two supernatural serial killers in love, versus a twelve-year-old.

"Don't touch that, thank you." Stacey said, measuring my eyeline towards the balestra. "I'd hate to kill you before the big reveal."

She began to chant words in a language I couldn't understand. The blue light that poured from her eyes glowed brighter, even brighter than the bulb that hung from the ceiling. The sound of a hurricane filled the room. I looked back at my balestra, but saw my axe had begun to twitch and jitter. It fell from the shelf, and bounced once, which was when Noddy fell out of my axe that he had been possessing, and fell into the murky water.

Stacey continued chanting. Her hair was whipped around her face by an invisible force, as she brought the heads of the two figurines down against the side of the freezer, smashing them. Two identical spirits released ear-splitting screams as they left the confines of the statuettes. Stacey spun her hands in an intricate gesture, and the two halves of Richard coalesced into two balls of light that orbited in her palm. Lightning sizzled between them, followed by peals of thunder that deafened me in the enclosed space.

"Noddy!" I yelled, over the din, trying to get the little spirit's attention, but he climbed up onto the freezer instead. Stacey's gaze was fixated on the two balls in her hands. They were desperately trying to fling apart, like opposite poles of a magnet. Her chanting increased in its pitch and fervour. Sweat cascaded from her forehead as she tried to control the two spinning pieces.

Noddy tipped over and into the freezer, and he was gone.

Meanwhile, Stacey was wrestling with the two halves of Richard, barely able to control them. With both hands, she slammed the two crackling orbs of Richard into the face of the golem she'd spent years making.

The two orbs hit the golem, but then ricocheted off its flesh, and into the air.

"No!" Stacey screamed, and tried to pull them back towards her, tugging on thin strands of silk that drifted between the statues and the orbs.

One piece of the orb, blind and confused, shot past me and up the stairs.

Stacey looked between the orb hanging in the room, and then the staircase. She let go of the orb she was holding, and launched herself through the water, up the stairs, and after the elusive half of Richard that was fleeing.

I pulled on the shelf above me, and it collapsed like wet cardboard. The balestra fell, and I managed to catch it moments before the water did.

The golem sat up, and smacked his head against the rim of the freezer.

"Ouch," came the voice of Noddy.

He climbed out, shivering. The orb of Richard's spirit now flitted about the room like a spooked housefly.

"Are you okay?" I asked. My ears were ringing.

Noddy's eyes were empty sockets, glowing with energy. He pulled the tablecloth down from the shelf where Stacey had left it, and fashioned a toga to cover his new body.

"Kalauni would have been very disappointed, if I didn't stop that siren from creating a golem."

"So, you became the golem yourself?"

The tall, blonde rock star with no eyes raised one of his shoulders in a strange shrug. "Better me than whoever that Richard fellow was."

He bent down into the murky water around us, and then handed me my axe, covered in slime.

"I'm surprised you could even enter that body," I said.

"She must have been making a vessel that would accept any low-level spirit. I mean, look at it." Noddy gestured to the intricate stitchwork joining the segments of flesh, and the faint tattoos of red and blue that had been drawn where the tendons and veins should have been. "This is what? Maybe months of dedicated work?"

I notched a new bolt into my balestra, then I grabbed the dusty glass case of ancient books and handed it to Noddy.

"Let's beat it."

I slunk through the house from shadow to shadow, straining my ears to listen for Stacey's return. I poked the balestra around each corner ahead of me, sweeping the air between us and the exit. Noddy did his best to follow my lead, but as he walked, I saw that he had a profound limp. He held the large case of books in both hands as he waddled, dodging the broken nails and timber with his bare feet. We went through the house, past the rusted spiral staircase, and then to the front door.

We could have made it. Except the front door was rusted shut, and I should have remembered that. I unlatched it, and pulled.

The door swung inward as the metal of its hinges screamed, then snapped. The front door fell backwards on top of me, while I held onto the handle stupidly.

Despite the limp, Noddy was surprisingly agile in his new body. He dropped the glass case of books, and yanked me backwards, just in time to prevent the door from falling on top of me. The display case landed at our feet and shattered. In the relative quiet of that lakeside cottage, the sound would have been like someone ringing the doorbell.

"Grab the books," I yelled. I could hear the sound of something purring loudly as it tore through the forest towards us, crunching gravel.

Noddy bent down to collect the books, and we both went for the tiny window at the front. I rolled through first, and Noddy came after me, gasping as he trod through the broken glass that littered the living room.

"That's right. Glass beats skin."

He hobbled along the porch as I ran ahead to the car, keys in hand. I mashed the unlock button.

I was across the gravel driveway. I pulled the driver's door open, and turned the engine over. Something was screaming towards us along the road. I hit the headlights. The light leapt out through the early morning air, illuminating the dust that hung between me and Noddy.

Noddy was on the ground, and Stacey stood over him.

She held the lost half of Richard's soul in her fist. The sound of crunching gravel from the road behind grew louder.

"Off so soon?" Stacey asked. "I can see no one taught you manners. Let me guess, you went to a state school?"

"I was home-schooled," I replied, levelling the balestra over the window and at the siren.

"I see," Stacey said, with an apologetic tilt of the head. "That explains it then."

Noddy lay on the ground. He was trying to say something, but his mouth was full of dirt.

"The left leg is a little funny," she explained, and kicked it. Noddy screamed.

"I think it got damaged when I harvested it. Hard to run." She bent down and turned Noddy over roughly. "Now who exactly *is* this?"

Stacey was distracted, so I fired. I didn't hold my breath, like Grandma taught me, and the bolt tilted off-target as it left my balestra. A shot that should have lanced through Stacey's middle, caught her in the collar bone instead.

My hand reached for another bolt in my hoodie, but Stacey had already closed the gap between us. She was rapidly sucking air through clenched teeth.

Instead of loading the next bolt, I swung the barb at Stacey's neck, but she smacked it from my hand with the force of a cricket bat. I squinted through the tears as I hit the dirt, and tried to scramble back into the driver's seat.

Stacey picked me up from the ground, pinning me painfully against the car's door frame. In her spare hand, she held tightly to Richard's spirit. She bared her teeth, but paused. She was listening to something over the sound of the Mitsubishi's struggling motor.

A car with no headlights shot through the tree line, and swerved past us, peppering the air with gravel from its rear wheels. In the illumination of the Mitsubishi's lights, I saw Matilda behind the wheel.

She rose up and out of the driver's seat. Matilda's head vanished somewhere beneath her. Long, red tendrils cascaded to the floor below her, as her middle opened up into a ribcage of teeth and eyes. Her tentacle-like appendages collected Noddy's body, as well as the books, and quickly moved them into the back of the car.

Kalauni stepped out of the passenger seat, and cracked her knuckles. She didn't transform like Matilda had. That meant Kalauni was hoping to talk to the psychopath.

"Great," Stacey hissed. She looked back at me. "So, you were with the guardians after all."

I tried to choke out something witty, but my arms were trembling as I saw Kalauni step forward. Kalauni the mother, Kalauni the cook. Kalauni who hated fighting.

"Put her down," Kalauni said, walking confidently towards us.

Stacey backpedalled, still holding me aloft. "I'll crush her windpipe."

"And then what?" Kalauni asked.

"She's got some banned literature here," Matilda roared from the air above us.

"We've got your golem and your books," Kalauni continued. "Where does that leave you, and whatever plan you're hatching?"

Stacey licked her lips. I could feel her grip weakening, as blood dribbled through her blouse. She glanced at the car where Noddy and the books were.

I gasped for air.

"Alright," the siren said. "A trade then. You obviously care for this little piece of work—"

Kalauni continued towards Stacey, and she backpedalled again. My vision was growing blurry at the edges.

"—so, I'll swap her for the golem and the books. Nice and clean, cross my heart."

Kalauni nodded, "that does seem reasonable."

"Really?" Matilda's floating body called from the sky. "Why are you trusting her?"

Stacey lowered me. My toes touched the gravel, and I drank the air gratefully.

"Kalauni," I said through sobs.

Stacey released my throat, but held the hood of my jumper tightly. "I'm very trustworthy. In fact, I was school captain back in the day." She laughed. "I doubt you want this little snot to lose another adult in her life—"

Kalauni clicked her tongue once, in irritation.

"Don't touch my daughter."

Her hand seemed to wind-up from an impossible distance behind her. If Stacey was expecting the blow, she didn't react fast enough. Kalauni's bare palm smacked into Stacey's temple, and the siren's head detached with ease. The fingers holding me released their grip. I fell to the ground, gasping. The spirit of Richard unfurled from Stacey's grasp, and sped out into the forest, screaming.

Kalauni bent down, and I buried my face into her body as she held me.

"I'm so sorry," I said between sobs. "I should've listened to you."

"Look at that," Matilda roared.

We looked up, and saw what Matilda had spotted. Sailing up and over the cottage, Stacey's head was now falling like a shooting star.

"How beautiful," Noddy said.

We watched the head complete its arc, and drop into the lake with a splash.

* * *

Matilda was a maniac on the road, and had floored it past us as soon as she hit the motorway.

"How did you know we were missing?" I asked Kalauni, as she drove us home in the Mitsubishi.

"I've been waking up for the past three months to your night terrors," Kalauni replied. The orange streetlights lit her face over and over. "I jolted awake suddenly when I realised you hadn't called out for me."

"How'd you find us?"

"When I couldn't find Noddy, I went and found a great spirit who knows a lot of things."

"Ni ratted me out?"

"Yes, and I'm glad he did. We'll have to run a few odd jobs for him next week, however." Kalauni looked at Noddy in the rear-view mirror. He was staring down at his seat belt with empty eye sockets, and grinning with excitement.

"Don't get too comfortable in that body," Kalauni warned. "We'll have to turn it over to central, along with the books."

"Body's aren't that great anyway, Noddy," I said, and lifted my damaged arm to prove it.

Noddy raised his eyebrows, but then repeated the gesture over and over in delight.

"I suppose we can wait a few days before we return the golem," Kalauni said with a faint smile.

"It's just so easy to move around in," Noddy said, with glee. "Did you see me in that freezer? Stopped that Richard fellow when he tried to get inside this body. Woopow!"

Noddy was doing a terrible karate impression with his arms, which could now fully articulate.

"That reminds me," he said, and pointed to my balestra. "Your crossbow already had someone's spirit living inside it, so I had to hide inside the axe instead."

A long silence filled the car after that. I held the crossbow up to my ear.

"Grandma?" I whispered in the dark.

About the Author

Jonathan Furneaux (pronounced: "fur-no"), is an author and educator in Brisbane, Australia. In the second grade, his teacher let him write novels in the back of his mathematics exercise book instead of learning his times tables. As a result, he developed a joy of writing and literature, as well as an awkward pause before having to do any kind of counting.

Jonathan was awarded a High Commendation by the Fellowship of Australian Writers (QLD) for his first published short story: *The Second Father.*

Visit **www.jonathanfurneaux.com** to get some free stories, read his blog and reviews, learn about his future projects, and quickly find his social media handles.

Other Books

Lessons from the Wreckage is Jonathan Furneaux's debut science fiction novel. He has also co-authored a non-fiction chapter in *The Contribution of Fiction to Organizational Ethics* (2014), where he argues that Star Trek can teach you how to make ethical business decisions.

www.ingramcontent.com/pod-product-compliance
Lightning Source LLC
Chambersburg PA
CBHW022203170626
46807CB00005B/2329